HAINT COUNTRY

HAINT COUNTRY

Dark Folktales from the Hills and Hollers

Adapted, collected, and edited by
MATTHEW R. SPARKS
& OLIVIA SIZEMORE

Illustrated by Olivia Sizemore
Foreword by Jordan Lovejoy

Copyright © 2024 by The University Press of Kentucky

Scholarly publisher for the Commonwealth, serving Bellarmine University, Berea College, Centre College of Kentucky, Eastern Kentucky University, The Filson Historical Society, Georgetown College, Kentucky Historical Society, Kentucky State University, Morehead State University, Murray State University, Northern Kentucky University, Spalding University, Transylvania University, University of Kentucky, University of Louisville, University of Pikeville, and Western Kentucky University.
All rights reserved.

Editorial and Sales Offices: The University Press of Kentucky
663 South Limestone Street, Lexington, Kentucky 40508-4008
www.kentuckypress.com

Cataloging-in-Publication data is available from the Library of Congress.

ISBN 978-1-9859-0096-7 (hardcover : alk. paper)
ISBN 978-1-9859-0097-4 (pbk. : alk. paper)
ISBN 978-1-9859-0099-8 (epub)
ISBN 978-1-9859-0098-1 (pdf)

This book is printed on acid-free paper meeting the requirements of the American National Standard for Permanence in Paper for Printed Library Materials.

Manufactured in the United States of America

For Byron Sizemore and Carl "Junior" Fox

CONTENTS

Foreword by Jordan Lovejoy   xi
Introduction by Matthew R. Sparks   1

I. HAINT TALES

The Last Miner of Hurricane Creek   9
A Harlan County Séance   11
The Headlight Haint   14
The Phantom Playmate   16
"It Was Always On When They Needed It Most"   18
The Snowy Night Visitation   20
The Ghost of Fish Creek   22
"Robert"   24
The Dance   27
The Man in Black   28
Babies under the Floorboards   31
The Old Owsley County Jail   32
The Ghost Light   35
The Bloodstained Mother of Bailey Branch   36
The Crying in the Night   38
"Yoo-Hoo, Mary Jane!": Memoirs about a Haint   40

II. BOOGERS

That's How Grandpa Quit Gambling   63
"They Could Hear It Scream"   65
The Hellacious Beast of Wild Dog Road   69

Boogers of Harvey Bend, Part 1: The Sasquatch of 476   72
Boogers of Harvey Bend, Part 2: The Lady in White   74
"Cornhusk"   76
"Big Redeye"   80
The Fourseam "Thing"   83
The Phantom Beast of Cow Creek   84
The Lurker in the Cave   87

III. STAINED EARTH
"I Know There Are Spirits There"   93
Tales from Bonnyman Coal Camp   98
The Restless Spirits of Beech Fork Elementary School   100
My Haunted Double-Wide   106
The Old Hyden Elementary Gym   110
"Sam"   113
"A Soul Left to Wander"   116
Haunted Antebellum Property in Jackson County   118
"Evil Hanner" and the Legend of Blood Rock   120
The Spirit Drums   123
The Wrong Side of the Law   125
Chaney's Knob   127

IV. HIGH STRANGENESS
"A Thinness, Where Things Can Bleed Through"   131
The Hairy Arm   134
"Do You See That?"   136
"You'd Think There'd Be Blood Somewhere"   138
Being a Caul Bearer   140
"And I Ain't Been Back Since!"   142

"Witchy" George Joseph   *144*

The Unrest of Octavia Hatcher   *146*

How to Become a Witch   *148*

Another Formula for Becoming a Witch   *152*

The Legend of the John Asher's UFO   *154*

V. HUMOROUS HAINTS

A Successful "Haint Hunt"   *165*

The Pack Peddler's Bones   *167*

"That's the Closest I've Come to an Encounter with a Haint!"   *169*

Paw Hensley and the Naked Haint Woman of Squabble Creek   *171*

Afterword by Olivia Sizemore   *180*

Acknowledgments   *183*

Compendium   *185*

About the Authors   *197*

FOREWORD

When we think about where folklore and folktales might still exist, we often imagine rural areas, these isolated places home to people who have somehow managed to maintain traditional ways of life despite increasing influences from modernization, industrialization, and globalization. In historical and contemporary times, especially within the United States, folklore is often coupled with regions like Appalachia and our narrow social imaginary of it as separate and ever-rural—sometimes quaint and romantic, sometimes regressive and problematic. This coupling of the Appalachian region with a simplified idealization of American folklore (as something that exists primarily in the past) comes from a long, fairly straight path. The English term *folklore* was coined in the mid-1800s, and it originally was used to describe "popular antiquities," stories from those people who were believed to exist outside the reaches of modernity, outside of what was considered "civilized society." As the concept of folklore and the study of it evolved, collectors came to see it as quickly vanishing traditions of "low-culture" groups who still held customs and knowledges that more "advanced" or "modern" groups had outgrown. And those traditions had to be collected and preserved as quickly as possible, because they were at risk of disappearing; they also came to serve as romanticized relics of a past way of life that might provide escape for more urban, wealthy, and white populations to construct an intentional, often exclusive, idea of what makes up the "American" identity.

But folklore serves a much larger purpose in our lives than simply existing as quaint forms and traditional ways of life and knowledge somehow untouched by modernity. In reality, folklore is not merely vanishing traditions and stories from isolated, rural, and predominately white places; it is artistic, traditional, and informal culture that we pass along to each other through our small groups, and we dynamically shape—and reshape—it through our interactions across time and space. Folklore is expressive culture; it is lively and has continued use, dynamic variation, and transformative emergence in our everyday lives, including in Appalachia (as well as everywhere else). We are all part of the *folk* in some way, especially as we interact in our small groups, and we all have *lore*, forms of expressive culture, to share as we make sense of the world around us.

There are many different forms of folklore, which can be broken down into a few categories: material lore, verbal lore, and customary belief and practice. Material lore is related to things we make, things we can touch, such as vernacular architecture, baskets, quilts, masks, and costumes. Verbal lore is related to what we say or what we tell, such as jokes, proverbs, riddles, personal narratives, and urban legends. And customary belief and practice is related to what we do or enact and believe, such as rituals, dances, celebrations, superstitions, and myths. Often, these categories overlap or leak into one another. While many of the tales we might consider verbal lore are told and shared by word of mouth, for example, they might also deal with belief. This overlap between telling a story and believing a story is one of the focuses of this collection of haint country tales, which all have been told by word of mouth across eastern Kentucky and are now being recorded and shared in this book.

Perhaps most prevalent for the tales in this collection is the category of belief lore. While we often encounter the concept of belief in our daily lives through religion and spirituality, whether in groups or on a personal level, we also experience belief through folklore, through superstitions, myths, legends, rumors, gossip, and even conspiracy theories. When told one, do you believe a legend is true or that a rumor is not made up? Maybe your friend tells you a story of a human-animal creature frequently spotted in the woods, on trail cameras, and by locals that has glowing red eyes, claws, and horns and walks on two feet. Do you automatically question the truth of a tale that starts with the words,

I heard...? Do you believe a story that has been told and passed along by word of mouth in a specific place for years even if it seems unbelievable at times?

Many folklorists have noted recognizable features of telling belief-based stories; you might notice linguistic or verbal cues that belief—and the negotiation of it—will be present in the story you are about to be told. If a teller begins the story with doubt, for example—"You might think this is wild, but..." or even "You aren't going to believe what I heard..."—you might automatically listen with suspicion. One of the most common features in a story where belief might be debated is the "friend of a friend": "My uncle Joe's buddy, Freddie, told me..." The farther away the narrator of the story is from the story being (re)told, the higher the likelihood that a listener might feel skeptical about the story's validity. If you introduce an element of what might be considered impossible, unproven, or unlikely by your local community or the wider world (like flying saucers, cryptids, or even that the seemingly happy couple down the street is having marital issues), you also introduce the possibility—and negotiation—of belief. That negotiation of belief, the contestation of validity, and the debate over truth—"Is this fact, fiction, or something in-between?"—are hallmarks of legends, rumors, and ghost stories especially. You will likely see these features in many of the stories you read here. Still, it is important to note that just because belief in a story might be contested or questioned by its tellers and listeners does not mean that story is unimportant, untrue, or wrong. Noting the features of belief in a story is less a value judgment of the story itself and more a noticing of the work the story and its narrative structure are doing. And, to many folklorists, the work of a story as it is shared and the relationship between tellers and listeners are some of the most interesting parts about telling stories. For me, especially in relation to this collection of haint tales, the relationship between stories and place is one of the most interesting things to see.

How such stories are told and heard is also important for understanding the relationship between place and culture.

Because folklore is still often perceived as deeply tied to the past and the unmodern, it is often connected in our popular imaginary to rural places like Appalachia. Appalachian Dialectical English faces a similar perception in the American imaginary, as writers stretching back to the late nineteenth century sought to frame people and their language in the region as frozen in time. This framing gave rise to the misconception that English in Appalachia is a survival of Elizabethan English, preserved by the rural, isolated mountains and the poor white communities living within them; these framings have unfortunately supported the racist erasure of diverse experience and language use in the region, creating space for white supremacists to intentionally spread misinformation about some pure form of English in Appalachia untouched and uninfluenced by "outside" speakers, which of course does not exist. In reality, both folklore and English in Appalachia are varied and diverse, dynamically evolving as people use and transmit them, and you will find some of that complex language variation expressed in the tales of this collection.

As we have seen, migration, popular media, and the effects of modernization exist in rural places too, and the stories we tell about and within places like Appalachia often reflect the very complex and dynamic relationships among people, culture, place, tradition, and modernity. Take some of the tales in this collection, for example. Ghosts of miners killed underground walk through a local school, sites of Civil War battles leave violent traces in the woods, and unidentified flying objects appear over strip-mined mountains. All of these stories emphasize the negotiations between and effects of our modernizing systems and approaches that affect our lives and places—whether positive or negative. Folklore and the folk who share it exist in rural places and regions like Appalachia, just as folklore and the folk groups who transmit it exist everywhere. Whether in small towns or in big cities, in the woods or in office buildings, folklore's existence and emergence is not inherently tied to specific places like rural communities; it is tied to people, to the folk. Sometimes, then, people may share folklore (like haint tales and legends) about and within their places, and those stories might tell us a little about the place that story emerges from and continues to be told within.

Culture is of a people and often of a place, and that connection between culture and place is strong in the Appalachian region and communities within it, like in eastern Kentucky. As you will see in these tales, many of the stories we tell about place are deeply connected to both our past and our future—both reckoning with its uncertainties and imagining its consequences. Our stories can reveal our relationship with the past, the future, and place, but they also can reveal our imaginings, our visions, for the future through our current desires, anxieties, fears, and connections. It is through the very curiosity, exploration, and communities bound up with storytelling that we might make sense of our place; connect with each other; and productively examine and imagine what has happened, what might happen, and what we would like to happen. As we negotiate our own beliefs and visions for life, community, and possibility within our places, we might turn to our stories, old and new, to help guide the way. Here, in the pages of this collection, you will find some of those stories.

Jordan Lovejoy
University of North Carolina at Chapel Hill

INTRODUCTION

Where is "haint country"? It's not a place you can easily find on a map. Perhaps if you head down US Interstate 75 (I-75) southbound and turn off onto the Hal Rogers Parkway, you're heading in the right direction—but it's difficult to say for sure. We're not exactly talking about a place you can enter into your GPS. Like the "Otherworld" of Celtic lore, haint country defies a concrete physical location, and yet it hangs like a gossamer veil over the hills and hollers of Appalachian Kentucky. Sometimes, without expecting it, you might become entangled within this ethereal web, and well—let's just say, you may be in for a wild ride.

Chances are, if you've heard of Appalachia or seen the most common representations of our culture, you might have correctly assumed that we're a rather unapologetic, gritty, experienced breed of mountain folk. This is "not for no good reason." For better or worse, in Appalachia the woods and the hills are the source of our livelihoods; our ancestors were largely coal miners, metalworkers, hunters, fishers, loggers, foragers, farmers, and 'shiners—that is, people who make and sell "moonshine," corn liquor in layman's terms. Furthermore, our presence in these hills stretches back countless generations. For example, the remnants of the Stone Box Grave Builders (a subset of the Mississippian Native American culture that flourished between the ninth and seventeenth centuries of the Common Era) can be found all over central and eastern Kentucky. More recently, the Appalachian Mountains have served as the fertile soil in which the stories of the many Indigenous, European, and African American cultures that have called these mountains home became entangled. These roots run so deep into the hills that over the years, we have coined our own term for a hybridized culture that has developed in Appalachia, *Melungeon*. This ethnoregional identity perhaps has the distinction of being one of the most ethnically mixed cultures in America. In recent years, *Queer-palachia* has also taken up the mantle of our culture in bold ways, and thus, the stories continue. In this collection, you will hear the cacophonic echoes of our ancestors in the voices of our storytellers.

Importantly, you will hear these stories as we would tell them to each other, that is to say, using our peculiar vernacular dialect, Appalachian English, and our language certainly is melodic, as you will soon discover. We've tried to provide definitions for some of the more important vocabulary for these stories, such as *haint* and *booger*, but you'll encounter others: substitutions of *they* for *there*, the droppin' of final *g* sounds, and other curious turns of phrase and diction that imbue these tales with a poetic quality of narration that "ain't" found in most similar collections of folktales. This collection, in a very literal sense, conveys the Appalachian-ness of the storytellers' voices, which ring like windchimes throughout the work.

As you may have gathered from our colorful history and the motley crew of characters who have peopled these mountains over the years, there isn't that much that most mountain folk have seen or encountered in the hills that is beyond our ability to handle—with a sharp mind and a bit of elbow grease. Nevertheless, these hills also hold many, many secrets. There are places in the hills to be feared as much as admired and above all respected, especially when the barrier between our world and haint country is thin. Haint tales, that is, stories such as the ones featured in this book, are part and parcel of our culture's encounters with the more supernatural side of carving a living from these hills over many generations. These stories, almost always passed down by word of mouth, serve as reminders that things are not always as they seem when we are out in the hills. Their purpose, above all, is to entertain, providing the same thrills that one might get from a modern horror film. However, their secondary purpose is to instruct, aiming to teach younger generations of Appalachians how to keep their wits about them if they should by chance stumble into haint country while out in the woods.

As you will no doubt notice while exploring these tales, many of them have common themes. One of the oldest tropes you will find in the tales of haint country is what I like to call "when the hunter becomes the hunted." Should you ever venture into haint country, you'll find that it operates according to a different set of rules than does the world we reside in. The laws of physics and the basic principles that undergird our reality seem to be inverted in peculiar ways. To wit, often even the most skilled and knowledgeable hunters in our region will come across fearsome otherworldly beasts that put them on the run for a change. Some of these creatures may resemble their earthly kin—one of our favorite critters is a large black panther that seems to tread the line between worlds on dark nights along lonely roads. Other creatures of haint country are humanoid, or at least vaguely humanoid—it seems we have our own share of Sasquatch-like beings in the hills. These "Bigfoot" types also tend to appear with some otherworldly characteristics, including glowing red eyes, the ability to become invisible, and a stench fouler than any evil odors of this plane. Other creatures are more abstract—dark primal forces that cannot be clearly seen. These can only be felt as a menacing presence on the tail of your four-wheeler or as a sudden weight on the back of your horse or mule. Although they are poorly understood, these fauna of haint country, or as we call them, *boogers,* seem to come and go as they please. I must admit, we really don't know why they are here, but we can't say that we're unhappy to have them.

Moving along from the boogers, many haint tales deal with very humanlike haints. These beings are of an altogether different nature than boogers. Thanks to happenstance or unquiet rest, they tend to stick with us. These tales describe the drama associated with living alongside lingering spirits—the victims of foul play, crimes of passion, feuds, accidental deaths, suicides, deaths in childbirth (extremely common in Appalachia until the turn of the century), and other untimely or violent ends. It does seem that the haint population of Appalachia skews female, but regardless of gender, or lack thereof, many of these stories deal with haints' attempts to communicate with the living, or more specifically, to make their presence known to settle unfinished business in this world. In many of these stories, haints attach themselves to physical spaces, including homes or areas that they may have dwelt in while they were still living. Of course, we have plenty of "hainted" houses, or lands where the earth has been stained by the energies of events, persons, or creatures at the unwinding of their mortal coils. Sometimes, these spirits find the closure they were not able to have in life. Other times, they never fully leave, though they may quiet down to better adapt to cohabiting with the living. Indeed, learning to live alongside haints is part and parcel of many an Appalachian upbringing.

Sometimes, though, the stories are just plain weird. High strangeness abounds in the hills—and, although we may not be Roswell, New Mexico, we've had our fair share of UFO sightings and unexplained lights in the sky. We've also got our share of witches, doppelganger sightings, and other examples of uncategorized uncanny phenomena that déjà vu and bad dreams are made of.

We also have our fair share of anti-haint tales, that is, stories in which common sense prevails over fear and superstitious behavior, and phenomena previously attributed to haints fails the litmus test of cold, hard reason. These stories, though flipping the classical haint tale narrative on its head, remind us that although we may face the unknown in the hills, it is imperative that we always keep control of our rational faculties and never lose sight of the forest for the trees. They also teach us that humor, another important Appalachian value, is so often the antidote to fear, and in many cases, the two are not always so far away from each other.

These are just a few of the themes readers will experience as they explore the accounts in this book. However, there will certainly be insights that readers will draw from their own experience in navigating their way through haint country, and nuanced lessons left to learn that even elude us "veteran" haint country explorers. After all, haint country is mostly populated by simple, ordinary folk, not that different from you or me, who just happen to occasionally find themselves temporarily waylaid by the spectral variety of hill folk. Our haint neighbors are a strange sort, with manners and customs different than our own, which we often have no choice but to respect—at the end of the day, we do share the same space.

The stories in this collection are accounts of moments when ordinary Appalachian folk have crossed back and forth between our world and haint country and lived to tell the tale. Telling these tales, in fact, is an integral part of Appalachian storytelling culture and has been most probably as long as people have lived in these hills. I remember, even in the not-as-remote early 1990s, long car rides through the mountains and long afternoons and evenings spent visiting neighbors or at my grandparents' house, begging for "just one more story." In those days, the creativity of the adults in my life truly knew no bounds, and some of their recollected, and more embellished, accounts are also recorded in these pages. Most of the stories in this collection represent the storytelling traditions of the counties in which Olivia and I grew up. Leslie, Perry, Owsley, and the surrounding counties are some of the least represented in folklore collections of southeastern Kentucky, and yet some of our storytellers are the biggest characters in the state, as you will soon discover. In addition to my father's contribution to the collection, told from my perspective, I heard a handful of these stories when I was a child. The contributions of the late Carl "Junior" Fox Jr. were two of my favorites, which he recounted on one of my many weekly visits to see him and his wife, Anita, when I was a young boy. Junior and Anita were two of the individuals responsible for fostering my love of the "Appalachian Gothic" as well as the mysterious and macabre more broadly. In many ways, this book was made possible by their profound impressions on my innocent mind, and every time I pass the old black barn near their property in Owsley County, I am met with waves of nostalgia and goose bumps in equal measure.

In addition to rediscovering stories we had heard as children, the work of collecting tales for this book took Olivia and me to some very interesting places. I gathered many of these stories during trips around southeastern Kentucky as a part of relief efforts for victims of the catastrophic flooding of July 22, 2022. Although the volunteer experience was a traumatic one, this aspect of it brought me back in contact with just how important storytelling remains as a form of therapeutic entertainment and connection with other mountain folk in times of great distress.

Collecting other stories involved a variety of methods, also adapting them to the printed page, which the tonal differences in some of the narratives may convey. Some were transcribed from in-person interviews and phone calls; others were written and sent as email and Facebook messages. Still others involved quite a bit of archaeology, such as digging through and listening to an assortment of family tapes and reviewing old family documents. In quite a profound moment, my research allowed me to hear the voice of my great-great-grandfather Hobert Miniard, telling stories to his family and friends. Although I had to decipher his raw, unfiltered, thickly accented mountain speech, I was able to put together "The Pack Peddler's Bones" from one of his stories. Suffice to say, the voices presented in this collection, though some are divided by quite large distances in time and space, reflect the many faces of the Appalachian soul dealing with one of the most primal emotions: fear. And boy, do we love to talk about it.

To sum it all up, it's more than a little hard to explain to folks living outside the hills just what these stories mean to us, but this collection represents a modern, or postmodern, attempt to do so. I hope that you enjoy this field guide of haint country and that, if you should ever happen upon some moonlit Kentucky holler at midnight, you might find yourself in some familiar company.

Matthew R. Sparks
Ben Gurion University of the Negev

I HAINT TALES

Haint—*Noun* The Appalachian Dialectical English term for a ghost, spirit, revenant, poltergeist, or restless undead. Derived from the term *haunt*, as seen in dialects of the wider South, such as Gullah-Geechee.

The Last Miner of Hurricane Creek

Told by Scott Melton

On December 30, 1970, there was a horrible explosion in the coal mine at Hurricane Creek in Leslie County, Kentucky. Thirty-eight men died that day in the worst mining disaster in American history. I was six years old.

Ten years later, I was sixteen and had just gotten my driver's license. I was very into music and had been visiting my brother and playing and singing until late in the night. I left his house about midnight in my Datsun pickup truck, which was a stick shift. I knew my journey would take me directly past the site of the old Hurricane Creek mine, and it always gave me a weird, uncomfortable feeling. Just as I passed by the old mine, I caught sight of a man walking beside the road. He was walking in the same direction as I was driving, so my headlights showed him from behind. He had obviously been working in a coal mine. He was covered in coal dust and dirt, his boots were wet and muddy, and he wore the type of uniform that I had seen many other coal miners wear. He had a lunch pail in his right hand and a coffee thermos in his left. He wore a hard hat with a faint light atop it to light his path as he walked very slowly up the road. There were no homes close to the old mine, and I remember thinking to myself, "Poor fellow has been working all night at a truly grueling and physically demanding job underground and now is having to walk all the way home!" At that moment, I decided to stop and offer him a ride—seemed to be the least I could do to help him out. Being a new driver in a standard-shift pickup, I glanced down at the gear shifter briefly as I put the truck in low gear to come to a stop. Just as I was coming to a stop, I looked up to offer the man a ride—and there was no one there! He was just gone! There were no trees, bushes, or any places to hide. There was nobody there. Needless to say, I got out of there pretty quickly!

Now, I knew a lot of people who lived on Hurricane Creek, so over the next few days I told several people about what I had seen and each one of them had similar stories to tell me of the ghost miner. When I asked if there could have been anybody working in a coal mine and walking home, the response was always the same: "There ain't been no mine open here since 1970!"

Was it a ghost I saw? Well, I can't say for sure. All I can say is I saw *something,* and I know I won't be driving down Hurricane Creek after dark ever again!

A Harlan County Séance

Anonymous

If you grew up in the very small town of Baxter located in Harlan County, Kentucky, in the 1960s and '70s, then you may remember the popular daytime TV show *Dark Shadows*. It was, by today's standards, a gothic soap opera that aired on weekdays. The show was about the wealthy Collins family. It featured ghosts, werewolves, zombies, monsters, witches, warlocks, and my ultimate favorite vampire, Barnabas Collins. For months, my two friends and I would run home from school each day and plaster ourselves in front of one of our family's TVs and watch the thirty minutes of *Dark Shadows*. Almost all episodes had a séance scene with a Ouija board where someone was always trying to contact the other side and, as expected, some supernatural occurrence would then take place.

One day after watching an intense episode, my friends and I decided we were going to hold our own séance. None of us owned a Ouija board, of course, but that didn't stop us. We had seen enough of the show to be able to draw our own, and draw our own we did. We decided we would perform our own séance in the back bedroom of my grandparents' home, where I lived. It was the darkest room out of all our houses in the bottom. We gathered in the room one late afternoon to put our plan into action. Now, mind you, neither my grandparents nor my friends' parents had any idea what we were up to, and being mostly from Pentecostal families, they probably would have tanned our hides good if they had known beforehand.

We all sat on the hardwood floor of the back bedroom with the Ouija board in the center of us, and we all held hands and began. We had discussed our program at length and knew what we were going to ask the spirits and who exactly we were going to try and summon. Specifically, we were going to ask if I was going to marry the love of my eight-year-old life, Tim; if Dina was going to get the bike she wanted for Christmas; and if Shyla was going to get to see her daddy soon. Furthermore, we were going to summon a sign from Shyla's dead uncle, who had gotten killed by a train a few years before.

Well, to our surprise, when we asked the questions, the homemade Ouija board never moved . . . that is, until we began summoning Shyla's dead uncle. We were fully into summoning her Uncle J. when we all stopped and stared at each other in horror, because we heard a train whistle blow like it was right on top of us, and the Ouija board then lifted up from the floor and flew across the room, hitting the wall! Then, my grandmother came running into the bedroom from the kitchen after hearing what she described as a "painful scream" coming from the bedroom, thinking one of us had gotten hurt. What she found was three totally terrified and crying, hysterical eight- and nine-year-old little girls, hugging each other like we were going to be taken away by some supernatural force, and a piece of cardboard laying by the wall across from us. Needless to say, our *Dark Shadows* watching ended that day.

What happened in that back bedroom of my grandparents' house in Baxter, Kentucky, I still cannot explain, but from that day until I left that house, I always got a weird, scary feeling every time I walked into that bedroom.

The Headlight Haint

Told by Olivia Harris

Here's a good one for you from Sizerock, Kentucky. It's kind of well known, and you could even say it's a bit famous up here. My cousin was a Marine, and he had been stationed overseas. A few weeks after being home, he went out one night. On his way back home from the outing, he stopped by this gas well on the way to his house, because it's usually the last place you can get cell phone signal up here. He pulled his car off to the wide spot next to the special area.

We had all heard spooky stories and rumors about this specific location, but we had always thought they were just rumors. The local legend goes that there was a woman and her newborn infant that used to live up on the hill where the gas well was. The woman was said to have struggled with postpartum depression so badly that she ultimately ended up taking the life of her baby—I don't know the details as to how. Folks around here used to say that if you drove by that spot at midnight, you could still hear the baby crying. We always thought nothing of this—we thought it was all just made up to scare us. However, that night proved everyone wrong.

While my cousin was pulled over at this location, his car shut off. He thought this was really strange, considering it had been running perfectly fine just moments before. He tried turning it back on several times, with no luck. Suddenly, his headlights—but only his headlights—turned on, revealing the apparition of a woman directly in front of his car. He described her as being beautiful and wearing a long, flowy dress. She had long hair and she looked "so real." After lingering there in his headlights for a few moments, she disappeared in an instant, and that's when his car started back up. This experience made such an impression on him that after he finally got back home, he drew a sketch of her to show everyone how beautiful she was. He was so startled and in complete disbelief of what had happened; when you grow up around here you hear all kinds of rumors, but you never actually think anything like this could be true. That night changed everything.

The Phantom Playmate

Told by Tracy Banks Shepherd

When I was probably about six or seven years old, my parents and my aunt and uncle had taken me and my cousin, who was probably about a year and a half older than me, to visit their friends. They lived just above the road on a hill in a trailer. As you pulled into their driveway on the left, there was an old, rundown two-story house. The curtains were blowing about the window, and there was just something about this house that drew us in immediately. Of course, we were told not to go down there, but, as soon as our parents turned their heads, that was the first thing we did.

We go in the old house, and my cousin and I started out by just kind of rambling around and looking at the old stuff in there. Suddenly, a little girl comes up to us and wants to play. Judging by the look of her, she was probably five or six years old. She looked just like we did, I mean, as far as, you know, she didn't look like an apparition or anything of that sort. So, we played, and we played, and we played. Well, her mom comes out of the kitchen, which was in the back part of the house, and asked us if we wanted to eat, if we were hungry. Well of course, we were starving! So, she fixed us some sandwiches, and we sat down and ate on the stairs. These were old stairs, and to the left at the top of the stairs was that window that we saw the curtains blowing out of. We sat backward on the steps because this was an old home, the steps weren't boxed in, and we used the steps above us as a table, so to speak. We sat there, the three of us, with our legs backward on the stairs, eating, talking, and giggling. Outside, we heard our parents yelling for us to come on. We could hear my dad yelling at us to get back: "Y'all wouldn't supposed to be in there!" and all that. So, we tell the little girl we have to leave. When we got back outside, we told our parents, "You know, we've been playing with this little girl," and they were like, "Y'all are crazy, no one has lived in that house for years and years and years," since they could even remember, and "There definitely wouldn't have been a woman who cooked for y'ens!"

For years, my cousin and I have talked about this story, and we never knew if there was a backstory to the house or if there was anything to the story at all, when it comes to relating to a specific family or events that may have taken place there. This house was right off the main road of Highway 421. The house has been gone now for years and years; at some point it burned to the ground. So, who can tell if we will ever solve the mystery of what happened there? And what ever became of our phantom playmate?

"It Was Always On When They Needed It Most"

Told by Keisha Morgan

My mom used to tell us this story from when she was little. She, her brother, and her cousin used to wait for the school bus together at the mouth of the holler where they lived down the river. Every morning, they'd walk to their Aunt Flawre's house and wait for the bus, that way they didn't have to wait on the road in the dark. She'd always leave the porch light on for them, and sometimes she'd leave snacks or biscuits or something, too. They were the first people to be picked up on the bus route in the morning, so it was always dark, and it was nice to get to sit on her porch and wait by the porch light instead of having to stand in the dark.

Well, Aunt Flawre was old, so of course she died before they were old enough to be out of school. No one ever did move back into her house, and over the years the "earth just took it back," as my mom would say, but the porch light would still be on some mornings. Not all of them, mostly just the ones where there was no moonlight or anything, or the mornings when the walk there just felt a little more uneasy. They never did figure out how or why it would be on, but it was always on when they needed it most.

The Snowy Night Visitation

Told by Tracy Banks Shepherd

I'm going to go ahead and start with saying, growing up we were poor, but we never "went without," if you understand what I mean. Especially with my extended family, my mom's sisters and brothers-in-law and such. My parents divorced when I was five, so I spent a lot of time with my aunts and uncles. My aunt and uncle lived in a house that was very, very old. There was always a creepiness to that old house.

It was snowing that night, and the moon was shining so bright that you could see the snowflakes coming in between the cracks and planks in the house. The moon was the only light in the old house that night, and there was probably four or five inches of snow on the ground. All four of us children were in the same bed, with a pile of them old quilted blankets on us, in the same room as my aunt and uncle, who was in their bed. We hear a noise, and the back door flies open. This is a small house; there is one door that goes through and then on out to the next one.

My uncle gets up and looks, and there's snowy footprints going right through the house. All the way through the house. He gets up and walks out to the back of the house, where there was a ladder propped up on the outside wall. The steps that went down from the back door led out to the small backyard. The old wooden ladder had been propped up against that old house for as long as I could remember—it was pretty much rotten, with green moss on it, and only a few of the small steps were barely sound enough to stand on. I don't even know why it was there, but that was considered the backside of the house. He walks out there, and the footprints just went a few small steps up the ladder, and then they were gone. My uncle Charlie is a big man, and he tried to see where the footprints went in the snow and couldn't see. The ladder couldn't hold his weight more than a few steps up without trying to break. There was no explanation for what happened, or what kind of visitation we had on that snowy night. We never learned what caused it—'til this day, no clue at all.

The Ghost of Fish Creek

Told by the late Carl "Junior" Fox Jr. This story is dedicated to his memory and to his wife, Anita Fox.

In 1972, I took Daddy's champion coonhound, Mutt, and my other hound, old Buster, and loaded them in the trunk of my brother Glen's 1962 Ford. We stopped and picked up Lowell Gayle Morris, Gerald Moore, and Donnie Edwards. I wanted to turn the dogs out at a cornfield on Fish Creek in Owsley County.

After we'd been there about ten minutes, we heard a noise on the gravel road. We all looked up and saw a woman in a long, flowing, white dress, with long black hair fluttering in the wind, floating above a house across from the cornfield! Everybody grabbed for a car door, trying frantically to get into the car! We finally got everyone in—I think I had to drag a few, before I pulled over at a wide spot in the road to pick up the dogs. When we got the dogs, we hightailed it out of there, and though over the years I've been hunting at Fish Creek many times, I never look in the direction of that house!

"Robert"

Told by Tracy Banks Shepherd

When my youngest daughter was about a year and a half old, a close friend of mine passed away, someone I grew up with. He was killed in a car wreck. My youngest daughter had never met him; his name was Robert.

Three or four days after Robert died, my daughter Alicia started talking to what I'd initially thought was an imaginary friend. I asked, "Alicia, who are you talking to?" She said, "It's Robert," which, ya know, I didn't think a whole lot of it at first, because he had just gotten killed. We were talking a lot about Robert; maybe she had just heard the name—keep in mind, when my children were small, they could talk as plain as an adult, with the exception of just a few words.

Weeks go by, and we had kind of just stopped talking about Robert because the shock and everything had just kinda wore off. So, Alicia is sitting in the rocking chair, my recliner, and she's looking at a book that she's looked at hundreds of times. One particular page in that book would keep standing straight up, and she would smack it and say, "Stop it Robert!" And the page would lift back up. . . . Now I'm seeing this with my own eyes, and she would smack it down and it would lay down again. Then she would get mad and say, "Stop it, Robert!" and the page would stand back up again! Eventually, she got so mad she'd just start kicking and screaming and crying.

Fast-forward a couple days, she's in her room, playing. I'm cooking in the kitchen, and my kitchen is to the left of her bedroom. She's just, by now, close to two years old. She comes into the kitchen, saying, "Mommy, Robert hit me!" And I say, "What?" And she says, "Mommy, Robert hit me!" And I say, "Where," and, you know, was playing along with it. I was gonna kiss her boo-boo and send her back to her room. I thought, she's just playing with her imaginary friend, and she's nicknamed him Robert. She comes over to me, and I'm fixing to love on her and pay attention to her and all that. I notice she has a red mark on her face. . . . Now, it's not a handprint or anything per se, but it was a red mark. This is when I started getting a little more . . . alarmed, we'll say.

We go brush things off. A few more days pass, and she slowly stops talking about Robert entirely. We had freshly moved into our new home, and Alicia's swing set was out by the driveway, because our yard was muddy, and we didn't have any grass at the time. We were sitting in the kitchen by the dining room one afternoon; it's raining, and I decided to ask Alicia, "Where's Robert? I've not heard you mention him lately." Alicia runs to the dining room window and points to her swing set and says, "Robert's right there." And I looked outside, and the swing was moving, just the one swing, barely moving. I said, "Where? I don't see him." And she said, "Right there at the swing set." I said, "Ok, that's weird . . ." But we go along, more time passes, and she stops talking about Robert more and more. Which, you know, she's growing up; by now she's two and a half years old. Maybe she's outgrowing her imaginary friend.

A little more time went by, and one day I again decided to ask Alicia, "Alicia, have you heard from Robert? I've not heard you talking about Robert in a while." By now, about six months had gone by; I assumed she'd forgotten all about him. "Where's Robert? What happened to Robert?" I asked. "Down at the river," she said.

Now, that's when this whole Robert business really gave me the creeps. When Robert wrecked his truck and was killed, he was by himself. He wrecked over the side of the road, and hit a tree . . . down beside the river . . .

So that's where this story took the turn that, I felt there was something more than just her and an imaginary friend conversating. I felt there was some kind of connection going on and that Robert was coming through here channeling in some way, and Alicia, being an innocent little child, was picking up his energy.

My aunt has heard me tell this story. So, she went and told Robert's mother. Now, Robert's mother passed away just a few years ago herself, but she called me one evening and said, "Tracy, I want you to tell me everything." I said, "Fanny I can't; it's just a kid with her wild imagination. I don't want her to . . . I don't know—" "Please just tell me everything," his mother asked. So, I sat down on the bed on my phone, and I just told his mother, Fanny, this whole story that I've just now told you. She starts bawling crying, and she says to me, "That was Robert, that was Robert; that was his way of telling us that he's OK."

And I mean . . . that's really all I have to say about all that, because, that's basically where it ended. I don't know if Robert finally went on his way in Alicia's mind . . . I don't know. But that is one story that has really stuck out to me over the years. As far as like, seeing things with my own eyes that I can't explain, well, this is one I've witnessed myself.

The Dance

Told by the late Carl "Junior" Fox Jr. This story is dedicated to his memory and to his wife, Anita Fox.

In the early 1970s, me and a buddy, James Paul, went to a party one summer night, at an old white house by Old Buck Bridge, in Breathitt County. We walked in, and everyone there was dancing and having a good ole time.

I saw a pretty blonde girl sitting in a corner, all by her lonesome, so I went over and asked her to dance. When she stood up and I took her hand, it was ice cold. Chilled me to the bone. We danced. She smiled at me in a coy way but didn't say much. Eventually the party died down, and we went on our way back to Owsley County.

The next Saturday night, I went back alone to another party at the same house. I wanted to dance with that pretty blonde-haired girl again. This time she wasn't there. I asked around and described her to people, but no one seemed to know anything about her.

A while later that summer, I was out that way again and picked up an old man who was walking on the road. He asked if I'd take him to the graveyard near there. I did and got out with him as he walked to the grave he wanted to visit. There, on the headstone, was a picture of the pretty blonde-haired girl I had danced with at the party. The old man said, "That was my daughter, she died in an accident, on the way to her high school prom." I didn't tell him she finally got to dance.

The Man in Black

Told by Amanda Jones Smith

McKenna, when you was about two or three years old, what would happen when it was thundering and lightning out?"
"A mean old man in black would come to visit me."
"Why did the thunder and lightning scare you though? Why did you scream every time and say, 'Dale is coming'?"
"Because when he'd come, he would take my toys."
"And what did he look like?"
"He was solid black, and he wore a black trench coat."
"And he looked like the man you saw in the war book, didn't he? You picked him out, right?"
"Mhm."
"How many people in the holler here has seen him?"
"Three, four, maybe five."
"And what eye did you always see him out of, how did most people say they saw him?"
"Out of the left eye."

Who is the Man in Black? Everyone on Bear Holler up Rockhouse has seen him, and has asked this question for many years, decades even, before I was born. Some of these people won't speak up about it too much or would prefer to remain anonymous, but the Man in Black has been seen by some very well-known people in Leslie County.

When my little girl McKenna started being able to talk and walk, she would start crying and say that there was a man by the name of Dale trying to take her baby dolls. The only time McKenna saw Dale was when it was thundering and lightning outside. She also said she could only see him out of her left eye.

She was at my sister's house one night when a big thunderstorm came, and my sister called and asked, "Who is this person she is talking about? Who is Dale? And to this day, we have no idea who Dale is. We don't know if Dale is the Man in Black or if he is just another mysterious ghost figure that lives up Bear Holler. However, Dale is known as the Man in Black to us because at the age of two, McKenna said he had all black on: a black hat, a black trench coat, and his whole body was black. She said at times it looked like he had long furry hair on his skin—you could see the black fur on him.

The reason I know that he had a trench coat on was because one day I was going through a book I'd gotten from the Helping Hands club—I was a member and we had books that people gave to us to give out to the needy. Anyhow, I was flipping through the pages. McKenna about that time was about three or four years old, and she stops me and starts crying—"That's Dale!" she said when I stopped on one page. I looked at the picture, and the picture was of a Confederate man standing on a Civil War battlefield. He had a black top hat on like Abraham Lincoln's, and he was dressed all in black, including a black trench coat.

So, is Dale maybe a Confederate soldier, from the Civil War era, from sometime way back in the past, and his remains are buried somewhere in this holler? That's a mystery that we've all tried to figure out. I have tried to Google a man named Dale who fought in the Civil War for the Confederacy, but I've came up with nothing. But the Man in Black is for sure a real ghost figure who roams out in Bear Holler. People have seen him up at the head of the holler on their four wheelers and stuff. Interestingly, like McKenna, they always say they see him out of their left eye. He's been seen for many, many years. I'm forty-two, and the Man in Black has been seen before I came of age. But again, the Man in Black—it's fascinating to hear other people tell their stories, but I'm just trying to put the puzzle pieces together, and see if he is associated with who McKenna saw when she was a little girl. At about five or six years of age, she quit seeing him, and wasn't as afraid of Dale. I don't often bring it up, because if I do bring it up, she would be like, "Mommy, no, I don't want to talk about it," because it just takes her back to Dale taking her baby dolls away from her and talking to her during thunderstorms and all that unpleasant stuff.

Babies under the Floorboards

Told by Nathan McDaniel

Listen, there was a woman that lived up there in a house on Bailey Branch. She was a mean woman. Her name was Hanner Browning. She fooled around with men all the time, you know—different men. She was married, but . . . she had nine babies, and she fed all them kids to the hogs. Every time she had a baby, she'd take it out there and throw it to the hogs, and them hogs would eat that up. She'd stick a pin in the soft spot of their head to kill them.

So, my wife's grandpa and grandma bought Hanner's house. Jean, my wife, was still a young girl, and she said they kept hearing this baby cry. And she said her mommy, Rhodie, said that she crawled up under that floor, got way back there, and found a box. The skeletons of them babies was in that box. Rhodie pulled the box out with the baby bones in it and took it out of the house and buried it. And they never heard the crying again.

There's a spot on down below there, used to be Woodrow's place. Hanner's husband was going up the holler there, and they's a big rock out there. She got up on top of that rock there, her and another man. And her husband was coming up through there on a mule, and she shot him. He fell off in the creek and drowned himself. That rock sits right there. You go up there, there's forks in the road up there, and there it sits . . .

The Old Owsley County Jail

Told by Deron Mays

My first memories of the Owsley County Jail in Booneville, Kentucky, was when I was between my third and fourth birthdays. That would have been around 1957–1958. My dad was appointed county jailer when the jailer in office at the time decided to abruptly leave the position. In 1955, when I was one year old, my parents moved into the old Owsley County Jail from our small house on Route 30W about five miles from town. I was too young to remember the move. The older siblings recall those days, but my twin sister and I were too young. My first impressions were of being scared of the state troopers whenever they brought someone to jail. I would run and hide. I finally got to the point that I wasn't afraid of them, though.

The jail that we ultimately moved into is old today, but in the late 1950s it was less than thirty years old. It was built in 1930, I think. It replaced an older building that once sat in an area close to where this one was located. The jail was on Jockey Street, so named because it was the street where everyone tied their horses to the hitching rails when they came to Booneville in the horse-and-buggy days.

The jail was built from large sand-rock cut from a section of the South Fork of the Kentucky River that ran through the county. It had a full basement that had several rooms and a hallway. The living quarters had the same number of rooms and a hallway as well. The building had running water and bathroom facilities but no showers or bathtubs. It also had to be heated with Warm Morning heating stoves, of which there were three in the living quarters and two upstairs where the inmates were housed. There were two sets of stairs to get to the inmate quarters. The upstairs had one very large room, and inside the room were two cast-iron cages with bunk beds that the inmates used to sleep in. There were also beds outside the cages, and those beds were used much more than the ones inside the cages. There were two other rooms separate from the big room, and one of them was for female prisoners.

It wasn't unusual to hear noises throughout the jail. The cages had metal floors, and those would pop and crack and make creepy sounds. It didn't help that we had a theater just down the street, and they frequently had scary movies such as the highly popular Hitchcock films of the era. So, I was a little jittery to begin with at that age.

Several fellows have told some spooky stories about things they had seen, but I usually brushed it off as a result of intoxication or a hangover hallucination. One such story was from a couple of men who had been incarcerated for a few days. They claimed they heard clanging sounds behind one of the big cages. They had chosen to sleep outside the cages on cots to be close to the heating stove. The clanging sounds would get loud, then not as loud, until they would stop for a few minutes. Then they'd resume. After a few minutes of that, which they later said felt like an eternity, the clanging sounds were joined by a low, shrill scream, followed by a moan. Neither man was interested in walking around the cage to see what was causing the sounds.

Finally, one of the men got up from his cot and slowly made his way to the edge of the cage. There was about four feet between the wall and the cage, and that pathway was not well lit. He saw in the distance what he later said chilled his blood. In the back end of the cage next to the west wall he saw a figure, a headless man. When his eyes drifted downward, he saw the man was holding something. He finally recognized it was a head! The figure was holding his own head, gripping it by the hair!

He was so scared he couldn't talk, couldn't speak. He finally made his way back to his cot and told his jail companion what he had saw. He was crying. Both men jumped up and went to the front door, a huge metal door with a small rectangle opening to pass food and beverages and so forth through. The metal door was not very snug and could be shaken back and forth. They started shaking it and making a loud noise, loud enough to be heard from downstairs.

The family was in bed at the time, but we could hear the two men banging and shouting. I got out of bed and went to my dad's room, and together we went upstairs to see what was wrong. That's when we saw two of the most terrified individuals I've ever witnessed. They were both crying and begging for us to let them out and relayed what they had seen to us. Dad opened the door and walked in and asked them what they saw and where. The one inmate recounted his story. Dad walked back through the area he pointed toward, but there was nothing to see. He walked around both cages. Nothing. The two men were still not satisfied, begging Dad if they could come downstairs and stay in our living quarters for the remainder of the night. And Dad said yes. They stayed in the living room and slept on two couches we had. It took them quite a while to settle their nerves. They were able to get out of jail the next morning, to their relief.

I must admit, however, there were times that I had to be in the upstairs quarters by myself after that. I was about twelve at the time. Sometimes the jail would be empty, and I had to carry coal to the upstairs from the basement coalbin, which was another gloomy, poorly lit, and scary part of the building. I carried two buckets of coal up four flights of stairs to reach the upstairs and had to make about three trips. There were many times I recalled the night those guys told us about when I was in that room by myself. I never saw anything, but I did occasionally hear noises. I was scared. A story like that will cause the bravest of people to look over your shoulder at times. It will make your skin feel like it's crawling. I tried to block it out. The coal had to be delivered to the Warm Morning stoves, and that was my job.

I can't verify if the one fellow saw what he said he did (the other was too cowardly to look), but if I'm any judge of what a terrified person looks and sounds like, I know in that man's mind he saw something that night and it was very real.

The Ghost Light

Told by Shania Davidson

It was at the mine portal in Lynch. Me and my brother was driving through there heading back to Leslie County as it was getting dark during the summer. We were in a curve just down the road a lil' bit. We seen someone walking with a light that was dull and sort of flickering, so I turned my bright lights off to keep from blinding them, but their light slowly flickered out. So I turned my brights back on to be safe and not hit them . . . but there was no one there. It flickered once slowly, then three times, and then it was gone.

My brother got chills, and I laughed from how crazy it was. I thought maybe it was someone that stepped over the guardrail and went over the mountain down to somewhere, but it was just a hill and nothing at the bottom when we went back by a few days later during daylight. We even turned around and tried to see if anyone was back on the road that same night, too. We couldn't really tell what they were wearing, because they were just outside of how far my headlights would reach. I just seen the light moving sort of up and down like someone walking. It was aiming right toward us, walking toward us. It was a whitish, yellowish dull light and small. The flickering is what keeps me from thinking it was a phone light.

The Bloodstained Mother of Bailey Branch

Told by Sharon Shepherd

I was raised over in Bailey Branch and went to the old one-room schoolhouse up there. I heard this story from my grandmother when I was growing up. Supposedly, there was a young woman whose family was from up Bailey Branch, but when she married, she moved off to live with her husband's family, as folks tended to do. Anyhow, eventually she gave birth to a beautiful baby girl.

At some point, I reckon things soured between the young couple and the woman took her baby girl and left her husband to be with her family up in Bailey Branch. When her husband had found out that they'd left, he went up there to go get 'em. After a mighty row between them all, he either convinced or coerced them to return to his house.

On the way back home, they walked past the old Bailey Branch school (which I attended) and stopped so that the young woman could feed her baby. Bear in mind, the child was just an infant and still nursing. There was an old stone well beside the school, and the young woman sat down next to it so she could take a bit of a rest while feeding her little girl. I don't exactly know what instigated the next part of this story, but legend has it that at this point, her husband pulled out a gun and shot her dead. I don't know whatever became of the little girl, but the story goes that on some nights, if you passed the old Bailey Branch school, you could see the apparition of the young mother sitting out there by the well wearing a white dress, covered in blood.

When I was growing up, the old well had been filled in. But you could still see the stones that had covered the well, and that was probably fifty years after the murder had taken place. It was very spooky walking by that old schoolhouse in the evening. My best friend and I would walk by there but never go near the well on the side of the building, since everyone said that's where the lady appeared wearing the white, blood-stained dress. The poor thing is probably so lonely without her little girl.

The Crying in the Night

Told by Olivia Sizemore

When my dad was little, he used to spend a lot of time after school at Hyden Elementary, because both his parents were schoolteachers. His favorite thing to do was help the lunch ladies stock the kitchen, since they'd give him treats for his efforts. There was this one time he was helping one particular lunch lady who was a bit older. His folks just built a new house on Stinnett, so she asked him where about that was. When he told her they were living just after the mouth of Little Stinnett, she launched into a story.

Essentially, a long time ago there was a house on the other side of the road before you got to the mouth of Little Stinnett. It was a little cabin, and a husband and wife lived there with their baby. Well, one night, I think it was in late fall, it came a real cold rain that settled into a heavy mist and soaked everything through. The family must have turned up the heat to combat the cold, because somehow the cabin caught on fire, and the mommy and baby burned up. Apparently, it blazed so hard there was nothing anyone could do until the fire ran out of cabin to eat. The lunch lady concluded by saying that on wet, cold, misty nights, you could hear the doomed mother and child screaming and crying in the flames.

Now, Dad was a pretty inquisitive kid, but he knew grown-ups loved to tell tall tales, so he figured the story was fake. But one day, he was making his way to the creek across from Little Stinnett and decided to explore the overgrown field that shouldered the highway. Sure enough, there in all the weeds and grass was the old foundation of a house. He said it was even covered in black soot like it had been set on fire. He never said whether he had heard any ghosts or not, but it was certainly something he thought about often whenever he'd cross that field.

Even years later, when I was a teenager and the field had been developed with a number of houses, he told me the story as we waded by the area while dipping for minners. Looking into the backyards of the houses that sat there now, it was hard to imagine it as it had been. I'd never heard anyone else tell it, so everyone else who knew about it is probably gone. Surely the foundation had been destroyed to make way for the new homes, and any ghosts had gone with it, but I catch myself wondering. I often drive past the area now and wonder if anyone living there knows that old story. Maybe on cold misty nights, someone wakes up to the sound of a crying baby and wonders where the sound is coming from, only to be met with more squalling and the coming dawn.

"Yoo-Hoo, Mary Jane!"
Memoirs about a Haint

Told by Sharon Gibson McIntosh

On up Cow Creek from the Gibson place where we used to visit when I was a child was the farm of my mother's people. The family's name was Reynolds, and they had occupied that piece of land since the early 1800s. Grandpa Dudley Reynolds and his wife, Mary Moore Reynolds, lived in a house that had been built around one of the original log cabins constructed by the family shortly after their arrival on the creek. Much farming was done on their 444 acres, including raising purebred Hereford cattle. Grandpa really loved those cows. Part of the herd had been shipped all the way from Iowa, by railroad car and in the dead of winter, when my mother was a young woman. People always said that Grandpa cared more for his cattle than he did for most people—even going so far as to say, "If Dud Reynolds ever saw a man and a cow drowning in the river, he'd jump right in and save the cow."

Well, thank goodness that theory was never tested, but he surely gave the animals a lot of loving care and attention. When grass became scarce in the pastures in the late summer, he'd rent grazing land from other farmers, and he depended on my mother to help him drive the fat, curly-faced creatures from one pasture to the other. She was an excellent horsewoman, and he always said that he would rather have her to help him move them than any of his sons.

She had clear memories of helping to drive the herd from Cow Creek to Lower Buffalo Creek on several different occasions. A friend named Sherman Cooper had extra grazing land over there and was glad to share with Grandpa when late summer weather became dry and pastures were overgrazed. Mother often told us about riding up the branch between Meadow Creek and Lower Buffalo, never dreaming that she was passing the place where her daughter's and her granddaughter's families would eventually have their homes. If someone had told her then that she would build her retirement place there in 1971, she would surely have been surprised.

At the time she was frantically herding those cows by the farm where we now live, she was passing land once owned by George Fox, the widower of Mary Jane Reynolds Fox. Mary Jane was a sister to Meredith Reynolds, mother's grandfather, and had died a few years before the cattle herding began. Their big old house stood in the field on the west bank of the little stream. Mary Jane had died when my mother was five years old and had been buried up on the hill facing the Fox home place.

When we began to research Mary Jane's life, we were given a lot of information by various people whose parents and grandparents had lived in the neighborhood at the time. This is what we know: she was born January 13, 1848; married George W. Fox of Breathitt County; and had one child, a daughter, Nancy Elizabeth "Lizzie" Fox, born March 9, 1875, and died in 1937. Lizzie was a first cousin to Grandpa Dudley and was born the same year. She married Hycannus Ealey Moore, born 1873, died 1965. To the best of our knowledge, they were the parents of seven children.

It is said by old-timers that neighbors of the Fox family were concerned because George mistreated Mary Jane, was not good to her, and the couple had a lot of disagreements. On April 30, 1915, during a violent argument, George allegedly shoved Mary Jane, causing her to fall and strike her head, and she died from the blow a short time later. Everyone was of the opinion that it was an accident, but one and all agreed that her husband's actions had been the cause of her death.

According to people who were living in the community at the time, strange things began to happen at the Fox home soon after Mary Jane was buried. George Fox reported unusual sounds and peculiar incidents going on in his house, making him afraid to stay there. He told his neighbors that Mary Jane was "hainting" him, and he arranged to have her grave moved higher up the hill, quite a distance from the original site. A group of men from the neighborhood reluctantly carried out his wishes, and it was a difficult task, because the hill is very steep, and they would probably have had to carry the coffin all the way on their shoulders. Her burial site is still there, marked by a nice tombstone, which is nearly a hundred years old and beginning to show its age.

Mr. Fox must have been very disappointed after exhuming his wife's coffin, because the mysterious noises and extraordinary events in the former home of Mary Jane continued. They say that there was an upstairs balcony in front of the bedrooms, with a railing running along the length of it where riders would hang their saddles and tack at night. At times while folks were trying to sleep, some invisible force would clash back and forth along that space, causing the stirrups on the saddles to sway and thump against the wall. A noisy spirit of some kind would clatter up and down the stairs at night, keeping everyone awake. After a while, word got around that something mysterious was present in that house, and travelers hesitated to stop there even for one night. Widower George Fox had married again by this time, and it is said that the unexplained presence of whatever it was that had invaded the property began to be a real problem for the family. Apparently, that was when they left the farm. We haven't been able to learn where they made their new home.

After Mary Jane's house was vacated, a gentleman who lived in the area reported walking by the place and hearing a very loud racket emanating from the empty structure. He said it sounded like clashing pots and pans and cookery. A sincere and truthful man, he said he found the noise to be very troubling. From time to time, different families occupied the house, each having scary stories to tell. The building was eventually torn down, and the site remained vacant for many years.

In June 1962, Earl and I bought the Fox Branch property, and we moved here in October of that year. We were aware that it had once been owned by my great-great-aunt Mary Jane Reynolds and her husband, George Fox, but not once had we heard any of the plentiful tales about the events that had occurred there in the past. Later, while cultivating our tobacco on that plot of ground, we would often dig up pieces of broken dishes and crockery that Mary Jane had probably used and discarded many years before. A well that had been dug by the Fox family was still in good condition, and we could draw the most splendid, clear water from it—much tastier than the water from the drilled well that was piped into our house.

Later, when neighbors began to tell us of the old George Fox house that had been in the field and the accounts of the past, we listened, but I'm not sure any of us believed those stories. The men who built our house in the 1940s said that the stairway leading to our second floor had been removed from the old house. It is made of dark, polished wood. The spindles, banister, and newel posts are beautifully crafted.

As the years went by and our daughter, Andie, grew from a four-year-old child to a young woman, we made a lot of changes to the place. The house had just undergone a general renovation when we purchased it, but except for one old apple tree at the edge of the tobacco patch, there was nothing but grass and weeds growing there. Over the next years, we planted trees, shrubs, and flowers where once there had been none. We constructed sidewalks, outbuildings, and ponds, changing the looks of things and making it more homelike.

In 1977, when Andie and Ronnie DeBord decided to get married, we built a wing on the south side of the house, and the couple lived with us until about 1981, when their daughter, Carrie, was about two years old. That is when Earl relocated the tobacco patch so that they could put a trailer on the property, and they made that their home for some time.

In 1990, when the birth of their third child was approaching, they sold the trailer and began construction on a house, which would provide more room for them. Carrie was eleven, Matt was seven, and Jordan's birth was three months away when they moved back in with us while the building project proceeded.

We had a good time living crammed up together and working feverishly on the new house when time would permit, but space was limited, and the little family looked forward to having their own home once again. They hoped to be in the house across the driveway by Christmas, and we all made an extra effort to ensure that their goal would be accomplished. In the new house, there would be big rooms and plenty of space for the two children and the new baby, who had been born in June. The building project was not yet fully completed, but they were so anxious to spend their holiday there, they moved themselves and their few furnishings in on Christmas Eve.

Our house was strangely quiet that night, but theirs was bursting with noise and excitement, and toys and presents were stacked around a huge tree that wouldn't even have fitted into one of our small rooms. Remote-controlled playthings were high on the children's Christmas lists, and there were several arranged around the tree so they would be easily accessible come morning. The family settled down for the night—as much as any family can settle down on Christmas Eve. Andie and Ronnie had been asleep for some time when a strange noise coming from the living room awakened them. Andie got up to investigate and immediately called to Ronnie to come and look. Puzzling things were happening in there: remote-controlled toys were traveling unhindered around on the floor of that sparsely furnished huge room. When they would shut off the switches and go back to bed, the little vehicles would come right back on and begin to meander about, and this continued for some time until Ronnie finally took the batteries out so that they could get some rest.

In the confusion of Christmas morning, the night's incidents were forgotten until it was time to reinstall the batteries. Later that day, they related to us what had happened during the night, and none of us could think of a single explanation. Events like that absolutely could not have happened, but they did, and we were all very puzzled.

That was the very first episode of unexplainable events that were to come, and everybody remembers it well. During the next twenty-something years, even up to this day, there would be an absolute catalog of similar occurrences taking place. If you are easily scared, now would be the time to put this story aside. If you are a courageous soul and don't mind getting goose bumps and having other things prickling at your nerves, you are welcome to read on.

Nobody remembers exactly the schedule of incidents that took place. It probably was the television problems that came next. Not only did the toys continue to navigate about during the night, but the TV began to behave in strange ways. It would suddenly go off all by itself or come on at unexpected times. The family might be going out the door, and the television in the living room would suddenly come to life, and they would return to the room where it was playing, turn it off, leave again, only to have it come back on, with the volume louder than ever.

It was about this time that Andie and Ronnie began to discuss Aunt Mary Jane Fox and the stories they had heard about the old house. Could it be possible that there was something or someone besides them residing in their house? Maybe they should have thought twice before building a home on the same site where the supposedly haunted Fox home had stood. When they told us about their discussion, I, predictably, was apprehensive. Earl kind of chuckled—no change there—but the children were just interested and actually amused to imagine that they might be sharing their living quarters with a ghost.

Can you imagine coming to terms with that likelihood and still dwelling happily in the place? To me it was really unsettling. I had never wasted much time thinking about all the ghost stories that I'd heard in the past, but Earl had told me on several occasions, "There are things to be seen." Well, I preferred to not test his belief. I was happy with the here and now. There are enough problems with what you can see—without worrying about what you can't.

Every time the family across the driveway would go away for the weekend, I would have to go in the house to take care of the animals, goldfish, saltwater fish, and such; I would just hurry in, get the job done, and hurry out. Nothing could have convinced me to spend the night there. My little family was very content to live there and cared not one bit about the presence of whoever or whatever was in there with them. I, though, was content to stay on our side of the driveway as much as possible and leave well enough alone.

I remember one day when I was sent to fetch a karaoke machine from a bedroom closet. I didn't usually go any farther than the kitchen when the family was away from home, but this day I headed toward the back of the house and started to go into a bedroom, only to have the door close gently in my face. Now the first thing you do at a time like that is to look around to see if there's an air current moving through the house, closing doors and rustling papers, but the outside door was not open, the air vents were far enough away so that no door—I should say no door in an ordinary house—was going to close by itself. So, I knew that what had just happened was affected by some force that I couldn't, and had no desire to, see.

Definitely goose-bump time, but I had been dispatched to get the karaoke, so I cautiously reopened the door and hoped nothing touched the back of my neck, where my hair was standing at attention as I traveled through to the next room. I was able to find the machine they wanted and, thankfully, get back across the driveway. The door-closing thing happened to me a number of times when I had to enter one of their bedrooms; and the brave lady who cleaned house for the family finally admitted that she too had had the same experience—especially when approaching the doors to the children's rooms.

Jordan was walking very well for a two-year-old when Andie left to go to the grocery store one day during the summer of 1992, leaving Carrie to look after her little brother. While their mother was gone, the children walked down through the garden to our neighbors' house to visit and were coming back home when Carrie began to hurry along in order to get back to the bathroom. Jordan was taking his time playing with this and that on their journey, so Carrie went on ahead and told him that he'd better hurry up and follow. As she was about the leave the bathroom, the exhaust fan in that room suddenly began to just switch on and off, on and off, on and off, all by itself. Incredulous, she muttered, "What is wrong with you?" But it had frightened her, so she hurried outside to find that Jordan had fallen while crossing the drainage ditch and was unable to climb out. He wasn't hurt, just scared, as was Carrie, and she recognized that whatever was switching the fan on and off was concerned about Jordan's safety and was trying to communicate that fact to her. In retrospect, it did seem like the visitation of the mysterious being was always during a period of time when children were present in the house, and it never seemed that its being there was any threat to anyone; in fact, it seemed that it was actually trying to guard the family and its belongings.

Sometime when all the children were still very young, Andie did a portrait of them, using pencil and charcoal. It was a remarkable likeness, so she framed it and proudly hung it on the first floor, on the wall at the foot of the stairs. It stayed there for some time, and during housecleaning one spring, she decided to move it and put a new picture, which she'd bought, in its place. Satisfied with how the new print looked, she laid the children's picture aside and went through to the kitchen to clean up that room. She had barely got started when she heard a crash coming from the living room. Retracing her footsteps, she discovered her new picture lying flat on the floor—unbroken—just lying there.

"Well," she thought, "I didn't fasten it securely," so she put it back on the wall, making sure it was safely on the hook and went back to the kitchen, only to hear the same falling, crashing sound repeated. Annoyed, she went back in, again hung the picture in place, but, before she could get back to the sink, the sound was repeated, only this time it was accompanied by the sound of glass breaking. She discovered the whole thing lying in a heap on the floor. Glass broken, frame mangled. She said she couldn't help it—she gave a lecture to the destructive force that had destroyed her picture, slammed the old portrait of the children back on the wall, and, carrying the remains of her newly purchased print in her hand, she went back to work. There were no more sounds forthcoming, and the old picture of the children hung serenely in its place for years to come.

That was the same summer that the family took a vacation trip to Florida. They went, leaving Earl and me in charge of flowers, fish, growing grass, cats, and dogs. I went every day inside the house to take care of things, and I congratulated myself on my bravery. I didn't have any run-ins with mysterious things, and I was so relieved that everything had gone well.

The day that they were to return home, I walked cautiously through the house to make sure that it was neat and clean for their homecoming. The door didn't close in my face when I stepped into Jordan's bedroom, though I was about to discover a real mess. He had left toys and books scattered everywhere, and I thought Andie would be happier if she didn't have to come home to a room looking like that. It took quite a while to stash all the toys in the closet toy box and pick up the books and some odd socks and clothing that were lying about. I even gingerly picked up a rubber snake by the tip of its tail and put it securely in the closet with the rest of his stuff.

When I was finished, the floor was spotless, and the room looked a lot better. As I was placing a stack of his books on the shelf, I discovered that Jordan's baby monitor, which they always used to keep tabs on his every move, was switched on. They had been gone for a week, and the thing had been left on the whole time. Shaking my head, I reached to turn it off, and I don't know what possessed me, but I said into the microphone, "Yoo-hoo, Mary Jane!" The sound of my voice echoed all through the house. Smiling a little smile, I turned off the switch.

As I stepped away from the bookshelf, I was horrified to see the rubber snake, the very same reptile that I had just placed carefully in the closet, lying right in the middle of that absolutely clean, carpeted floor. The thing was still squirming from being hastily flung there by an unseen hand. How it had gotten from the toy box in the closet with the door firmly closed to the middle of the floor, I do not know. But I do know two things. One: I got out of that house as fast as I could move, leaving the snake lying where it was. Two: I have never, to this day, uttered another "yoo-hoo" to Mary Jane.

You may say that the concept of a ghost in the house is fascinating—entertaining, even—but highly suspicious. And you might even ask, "Has this ghost ever actually been seen by anyone?" That would be a yes. I'll explain. There was a cat that lived for a long time in the DeBord home. She arrived three or four years after the house was built. She belonged to Jordan, and her name was Abby. She was beautiful, had long black and white hair, and was not very large, but she absolutely ruled the roost. Stray dogs ran for their lives whenever she approached, because she would attack them with no warning whatsoever. Even our dalmatians, which we bred and treasured for years, were fair game to her. I never knew her to lose a fight.

One morning, I was on our front porch doing some housekeeping chore. One of the dogs was there beside me, when Abby came slinking across the driveway, scampered stealthily up the steps, and just launched her little self at the surprised dog. The intended victim jumped out of the way, and Abby sunk a lot of very sharp claws deep into my leg. She didn't mean to, but she had really hurt me. Limping, I shooed her back across the driveway and immediately called the doctor, because some of the family had seen her playing with the carcass of a dead bat that very morning. The health department shipped the bat to UK, where it thankfully tested negative for rabies; I had a bunch of antibiotics and eventually forgot about the incident; but you can see that this Abby cat was a real piece of work!!!!

As she got older, the DeBord family began to notice Abby behaving very strangely. She'd sit in the kitchen and look up in the air, just simply sit there and stare at what appeared to be nothing. Then she might follow, with her eyes, this nothing that she was watching as it apparently went through the wall and into the next room. She would get up, saunter through the door to that room, and watch as the invisible object made its way, through the air and through the walls, all through the house, and she would pad along behind it. The regularity of these puzzling actions increased. By that time, it had been accepted that there was, indeed, a ghost in the house, and they began to understand that the cat could probably see it.

Matt and Lalola Campbell were married by this time and had a young baby named Allison. The young couple came to the DeBord house one evening and left the baby with Andie to babysit while they went to a class reunion or some such function. Anxious to spend time with the baby, I traveled across the driveway and found Andie in a rocking chair, giving the baby her bottle. I made myself comfortable in another chair, and the cat came and made a nest in my lap, first carefully washing her face and then settling down for a nap.

Andie and I chatted about first one thing and then another, and suddenly I felt Abby jolt to attention. Looking down, I was amazed to see her looking intently at a spot just above and behind my head. Her eyes were huge and black, and she began to snarl and growl deep in her throat. "Andie," I whispered, "what's wrong with this cat?" She looked over at us, glanced up above my head, shrugged her shoulders, and said calmly, "It's probably Mary Jane. She'll be alright."

She'll be alright, I thought; Mary Jane, I thought—nearly frozen with panic. How can she be so casual about something skulking around so close to my head? But she just picked up the baby to carry her to bed, gathered up the pacifier and the other baby things as well, and headed up the hallway to the baby's room. Abby, the cat, shifted her gaze from the spot up above my head to a place just above the form of the retreating Andie. When Andie, the baby, and whatever was drifting around up there above them all disappeared into the bedroom, the cat in my lap yawned, stretched, flicked an imaginary piece of lint from her whiskers, and went back to sleep. Exasperated, I roused her, deposited her on the floor, said my goodnights, and headed to the house.

Nervous about my experience, I told Earl all about what had happened. I'm a fast talker when I'm scared, and he must have thought it was funny, because when I finished my story, all he did was smile and chuckle. It's hard to go to sleep at night when things like that are happening so close to your house and no one but you is even remotely concerned. I find this to be extremely disturbing! Don't you?

So, obviously, the cat could see the ghost. What about people? When Carrie's son, Cy, was nearing the age of three and just beginning to talk fairly well, he, his mother, and his sister, Brooklyn, were visiting at the DeBord house across the driveway one morning. Andie and Carrie were searching for something on the internet, Brooklyn was at my house helping to bake cookies, and Cy was playing in the computer room where they were sitting. They noticed that he was being particularly quiet, so Carrie turned to see what he might be up to. He was standing very still and staring toward the corner of the room.

"What are you looking at, Cy?" Carrie asked. He continued to gaze straight ahead and didn't move nor answer. "Cy," she inquired again. "What are you looking at?"

He remained perfectly still, staring at the vacant corner of the room. By that time, both Andie and Carrie were becoming uneasy, so Carrie spoke abruptly to him, trying to find out what was wrong. She didn't like the way he was acting. As though just realizing that his mother was talking to him, he turned with an awed but childlike expression on his face and exclaimed, "It's a ghost, Mommy. It's a spooky ghost!"

"A ghost? Where do you see a ghost?" Carrie knew that whatever he was looking at must be right there in front of them, but she didn't want to frighten him.

"In the corner," he said, pointing his chubby little finger. "Right there in the corner."

"What's it doing?" Carrie said, hoping to sound like it was something that happened every day.

"Nuttin'," he replied and shrugged his little shoulders. "Just standin' there."

"Is it a girl or a boy?"

"It's a girl," he said, and then, as though something or someone was about to exit the room, he turned and seemed to be following it toward the hallway that led from the computer room to the living room.

Carrie and Andie both quickly hurried after him. Straight to the living room he went, down the step and out into the room, where he turned his head as though watching someone go up the stairs.

"Is she gone now?" Carrie asked as casually as possible.

"Nope," he replied.

"Well, where is she?"

He pointed: "Just standin' up there on the stairs, Mom, don't you see her?" He sounded very annoyed by now.

"Unfortunately, no," Carrie muttered to her mother, all the while rolling her eyes. They didn't know whether to grab him and haul him to safety or continue to stand there with goose bumps assaulting every inch of their skin.

"Well . . . she's gone now," Cy suddenly proclaimed and headed back to where he had been playing.

Both women were wide-eyed and excited about their first visual contact with the ghost, but they did not want that sweet little boy to be aware of the fact. With raised eyebrows and hands fluttering over their hearts, they tried to go on with their internet surfing as calmly as they could. It just wouldn't do to make a big deal of it and have their baby worried about his discovery. Back at the house a couple of days later, he would be heard to call out, "Hey, Ma. Your spooky ghost is standin' up there on the stairs again—come and see."

Although Andie could not see what Cy was looking at, she wouldn't admit that to him. All she could do was amble into the room, look at the empty stairs, and say, "Well sure enough, there she is." And that satisfied a little boy and did not make him more curious than anyone would wish him to be.

Two weeks passed, and he hadn't mentioned the ghost again. On a Sunday, he went to visit his other grandparents and joined his grandmother at their family's church service. Entering the sanctuary early, they took seats and visited briefly with friends. Suddenly Cy began to tug at his grandmother's sleeve and whisper,

"Mammaw, Mammaw," with some urgency. Finally she allowed him to interrupt the conversation she was having to ask him what in the world was wrong.

"That lady," he whispered excitedly, "See her up there?"

"Yes, I see her, Cy. What about her?"

"She looks just like Ma's spooky ghost!!!" He seemed to be amazed but extremely pleased about his discovery.

Mammaw Carol had known the little old lady in the church all her life, and she memorized what she looked like that particular morning so that she could relay the information to Carrie: Small, slender, elderly, with gray hair tucked in a little bun on the back of her head and dressed as older women sometimes do, in a shapeless cotton dress. This is apparently what Mary Jane looks like. A child not quite three years old, who had just learned to talk and whose only experience with ghosts had been the cartoon variety, would never imagine, pretend, nor make up a story like that to astonish adults. Maybe when he was older he might have been capable of it, but not at the age of almost three. We believe that he has seen Mary Jane on two occasions.

On the evening of March 13, 2013, Ronnie came home from fixing somebody's heating system and sat down in his recliner to rest and to check his email while waiting for Andie to return from choir practice at church. Something caused him to glance up and, lo and behold, there in front of the lighted saltwater fish tank in the entryway stood Mary Jane. He told Andie when she came in that all he could see was a whitish, dresslike garment, but the head and extremities of the ghost were enveloped in what looked like mist. He said the vision lasted only a brief time and then vanished. He also said that he didn't move from that chair until Andie came through the kitchen door. He's never been afraid of whatever is in that house. He has one-sided conversations with it about the TV on a regular basis, but then again, he's never seen her before. We'll see how that turns out.

As I said before, the family does not fear this being, spirit, ghost, or whatever it is. It has never seemed intent on harming any of them. But there was one incident that caused Andie to be extremely afraid. In the early morning hours, one night in 2009, she woke up to look at the clock on the bedside table. There were quite a few electronic gadgets in the room producing their telltale digital glow, and in that faint light she saw something that really scared her. She said that there was a thick, rolling cloud of something like fog up near the ceiling. It was swaying and revolving, constantly moving but going nowhere. Scarcely daring to breathe, she watched it for a few minutes. Then she quietly woke Ronnie and told him to look at the ceiling. At first sleepy and uninterested and then immediately wide awake, he joined her in observing the mysterious sight.

"What in the world is that?" she whispered hoarsely while clinging desperately to him for protection.

He didn't answer, and his silence frightened Andie even more. Finally, he whispered back, "I . . . have . . . no . . . idea."

Together, they watched while the writhing, swirling cloud faded and finally disappeared. Ronnie went back to sleep, but Andie said she remained awake the rest of the night. It was the first time she had actually seen something ghostlike with her own eyes, and she says she still looks suspiciously at the ceiling when she is awakened in the middle of the night. They both maintain that what they saw was not the same as dealing with Mary Jane. It was something new and quite scary. They report that there are many times when they will catch a glimpse of something moving about the room . . . something that will just whisk by but is gone by the time they turn to look. They say that this happens frequently.

One evening, not too long ago, Andie wanted to watch a television program on the Hallmark Channel, but Ronnie had plans to watch something else, so Andie settled herself on the bed in front of the TV in their bedroom, and her program began. It was just getting interesting when her romantic story suddenly disappeared, and another channel took its place.

"Whatever . . . ," she muttered and pressed the recall button to quickly return to her station and so resumed watching only to have the same thing happen again, ending up with some other random show in progress. After several unsuccessful attempts to have her way, Andie threw the remote to the foot of the bed and snapped to the empty room, "OK, so you don't like romantic shows. What other one are you determined to watch?" The TV continued to play; nothing happened. After a bit Andie ordered, "Turn the TV to channel 1-8-5. I said 1-8-5." Unbelievably, on the screen, the numbers 1 then 8 and then 5 appeared, and Hallmark once again came into view. Pleased but also astonished, Andie finally snarled, "Thank you very much," retrieved her remote, and that was the end of that.

When she told me the story, I asked her if she was comfortable having things like that happen, and she insisted that it's much like dealing with a regular family member. They say that there's no way to tell how many times their TV will abruptly be turned off at ten o'clock, causing Ronnie to sigh and ask that it please be turned back on so that he can watch the news, and mysteriously it will be turned back on. Apparently, ten o'clock is a ghostly bedtime.

Other strange things happen regularly. A visiting family member may be feeding her baby its dinner, and that child will take a bite of food then lean and peep around behind his mother, who is wielding the spoon. There is nothing back there to look at, but the baby behaves as if he is playing peek-a-boo with someone and continues to lean and peek and smile with every bite, all through the meal, causing said mother to freak out, knowing what is probably causing the problem. Everything described here has happened—mostly to the DeBord family, but sometimes to others. My experience with this otherworldly being has thankfully been very limited, but nonetheless spine-tingling. Never before believing in the supernatural, I have come to agree with Earl when he says that there are things to be seen, not only in the house of Mary Jane, but other places as well.

As recently as March 1, 2012, I took our two Labrador retrievers and the DeBord family's German shepherd for their evening walk on our property, north of the house. Reaching the pasture fence, I paused with my elbows on the gate to watch the dogs do their usual sniffing detective work on the other side. While they ranged farther and farther away, I looked here and there, hoping to see some sign of spring, when my gaze finally settled on the woods above the pasture, and I saw a puzzling sight. At first I thought it was a plastic Wal-Mart bag. Transparent, almost white and oblong, it seemed to be about eighteen to twenty inches in length and probably six inches across, and it was just floating through the edge of the woods. I noticed that there was no breeze and wondered how it could possibly be moving along like that about six feet above the ground. While I watched, another identical object came into view a short distance behind the first, and then a third, all in a row moving from south to north. Instead of traveling in front of or behind the trees around them, it appeared that they were actually drifting right through the tree trunks. While I watched, all three dogs caught sight of them and began scrambling toward the woods to investigate. When that happened, the mystifying objects just turned and began to drift slowly up the hill through the trees, and they moved out of my sight.

I just stood there wondering what in the world I had just witnessed. Had I dreamed it? But, no—the dogs had definitely seen what I'd seen, or they wouldn't have been running flat out in that direction and barking their heads off. How I wished that I'd had a phone in my pocket so that I could have taken a photo to prove what I had seen. Unfortunately, that was not the case, so I hurried back to the house to tell everyone about it while it was fresh on my mind. The next day we watched media coverage of a horrific tornado that had struck northeast of us in West Liberty. Then we were warned that another had hit East Bernstadt and was headed northeast, directly toward us. The news reporting was continuous, so we sat, worried and apprehensive, ready to seek shelter, but the deadly storm seemed miraculously to just dry up. It simply disappeared and, thankfully, never reached our area. The following day I was talking on the phone to my brother who lives in Northern Kentucky. We discussed the storms in our area and also a deadly twister that had narrowly missed his neighborhood. We agreed that we were all very fortunate to have escaped when so many others had fared so badly. I happened to mention the mysterious objects I had seen the day before and wondered aloud what they were and whether they might have been a storm warning.

He was quiet for a moment, and then he asked me whether I had considered that they might have been placed there to protect and to guard us from danger. A shudder moved up my back. I didn't know how to answer him. That's an overwhelming concept to consider—to think that there are forces out there, sometimes seen and sometimes not, that are able to visit us at will, to protect and to guard or to just exist with us for whatever reasons we'll never understand! Folks who deeply believe in God, and I am one of them, put our trust completely in Him and appreciate that our lives are absolutely in His hands. That is so reassuring every day of our lives. What truly bewilders us, however, are the things which happen that cannot be explained. Who knows why that apparition is dwelling in the house across the driveway? How did it get there, and why doesn't it move on? What was the nature of the phantom shadow that sprinted down the road decades ago, on Cow Creek, scattering gravel and frightening a group of boys? What sort of unearthly creatures did I observe drifting through our woods, and is three a significant number?

Positive identification of the ghost in the DeBord house, of course, will never be made, but all our research and all the activities that we have observed and reported here have convinced us that it is most likely the spirit of Mary Jane Reynolds Fox. It is too much of a coincidence that this supernatural being was not heard from after the old George Fox house was torn down but showed up immediately, on the same spot, the day the family moved into the new structure. It is dreadful to contemplate that at death a person's spirit could possibly become misplaced, abandoned, or lost—much like being shipwrecked with no hope of ever being rescued. And why would a soul as gentle and benign as this one—as inquisitive and childlike as Mary Jane seems to be—simply fall through the cracks on the bridge to a better place? I'm certain that those questions will never be answered here on earth, but, in another life, possibly, all things will be made crystal clear.

Addendum dated January 3, 2015:

Early on Monday morning, September 29, 2014, Earl woke me, saying, "Help me . . ." Before I could get around to his side of the bed, he had become unresponsive and quite rigid. Perspiration was dripping off him, and I quickly grabbed the phone and asked Andie to come and help me. After a rapid trip to the Irvine hospital in a technically specialized ambulance driven by the fastest and safest driver I have ever ridden with, emergency room staff determined that Earl had suffered an abdominal aortic aneurysm rupture. A helicopter rushed him to the University of Kentucky Hospital in Lexington. Hours of surgery followed, but they were unable to save his life. The doctor said that the cards had been stacked against Earl at the outset. We returned home, after dark, red-eyed, stumbling, devastated and forlorn.

On their back porch, Andie and Ronnie noticed the hummingbird feeder was vigorously swinging back and forth. There had been a lone bird hanging around—it was September 29; hummers should have been on their way south weeks ago—so they attributed the action of the feeder to that little fellow and went on in the house. Back outside to feed the dog, Andie was puzzled that the feeder continued to swing rather wildly and without pausing. Too miserable to think about it further, she and Ronnie prepared for bed and spent a sleepless night.

Next morning, Tuesday, when the back door was opened, the first thing they saw was the birdfeeder still making its wide arc. While funeral plans were sadly being made and friends notified, the hummingbird feeder never once stopped its motion. First Andie and then Ronnie would get out of bed during the night to check, and it would still be swinging. This continued until Thursday morning, when at last it stopped. An incessant phenomenon occurring from sometime Monday until Thursday morning. As we struggle with this new life without Pappaw, we hesitate to even try to figure out what it meant, but we are certain that it signified something. Something noteworthy.

During the weeks that followed Earl's death, the children appeared regularly to gather together with us in an effort to obtain strength for us all. Something that we all began to notice was Jordan and his wife Dannel's twenty-eight-month-old son as he would play in the living room of the DeBord house. The ceiling is really high, and there is a vast space up above the actual area where sofas and chairs are scattered about. As he would play with various toys, he began to regularly look up at that vacant spot above our heads and smile shyly, holding up a toy to be viewed from above. This continued for several days. We all noticed but didn't question him because we felt that Mary Jane might be up there keeping watch over the child as she has a way of doing. Finally, his father had had enough of the mystery.

"Carlisle," he said quietly as his son was playing and smiling sweetly toward the ceiling. "Where's the lady?"

In answer, the child pointed his little finger upward and smiled as if to say. "She's right there, Dad."

Confusion triggers research, but try as we may, none of us have ever been able to solve the continuing mystery of things that happen here on the Fox Branch of Meadow Creek.

II

BOOGERS

Booger—*Noun* Appalachian Dialectical English term for a monster, cryptid, or otherworldly beast.

That's How Grandpa Quit Gambling

Told by Rhonda Turner Meade

Okay, this is a story that my grandmother told us about the night that the Devil himself chased my grandfather. My grandfather liked to gamble, and my grandmother was religious, and she didn't like for him to gamble—she liked for him to stay home with her and the kids. But, oftentimes, he'd do just that. He'd leave them to do on their own, and he'd go out to gamble. After a few rounds of card games, he'd start home, which was quite a ways.

One such night, after he had left the gambling house, he started walking back home, 'cause everybody walked back then—they wasn't no transportation—and he heard footsteps behind him. He turned to look around, and there was nobody there. So, he started walking again, still hearing those footsteps behind him. He turned around, and again, nothing was there. So, he started walking faster, and the footsteps started walking faster to keep up with his pace. The faster he walked, the faster the footsteps came—'til he started running! And he ran and ran as fast as he could; he just didn't think he could make it to the house fore whatever it was a-chasin' him; it was hot on his tail, and soon it would surely overtake him!

But, somehow, he managed to get back to the house, threw open the door, and slammed it behind him without taking a second look back! He told my grandmother that it was the Devil himself who chased him home and that he would never, ever leave the family to go out and play cards again!

"They Could Hear It Scream"

Anonymous

When I was very little, we would spend the night at Grandma June's. There were some weekends that the aunts and the cousins would all pile up in the car and we would just go up there to stay. One night when we were staying over there, the electricity went out, and all the cousins started crying because all the lights were out. The mothers made the decision to pile all the kids into the living room on blankets and pillows, and the adults stayed in there with us for a little while, until we started nodding off; they would talk and tell us stories until we'd go to sleep.

So, they started talking and telling the usual little ghost stories that you'd hear in these parts as a kid, like "Who's Got My Golden Toe" or whatever. This particular storytelling session eventually led to someone asking: "What about the one with the panther? Ain't there a black cat like a black panther that would be in the woods?" Basically, just a scary big cat story. Now, this subject created a big back-and-forth between the adults. "Oh, I don't believe that," one of the aunts said. "There's never been any such thing." Then another one of the aunts said, "Mommy, what about you? What kind of stories did you hear about it?"

Grandma June then recounted: "Very often, we would hear of people going from this holler or this part of the creek to another and feeling like they were being watched. This happened especially at night, and especially when they were on horseback or a mule." Grandma then said that there was someone that she knew specifically, and I don't know if it was one of her cousins or one of her brothers, who was riding through the holler one night and they could hear "it," whatever it was, jumping from tree to tree above them as they were trying to coax their mule on down the

road, which was really just a rough path through the woods. As they were coming up near the end of that part of the creek where they were going to move into a wider area, they eventually got their mule trotting along, but they could still hear "it" swiping its big paw, and they could feel the whoosh of air from it passing over their head. Then they heard it scream, and they said it sounded just like a woman screaming.

Now, here's my take on that. When we lived up at the old house, Shelly, Ernen, and I were playing back by the canning house on that side of the yard. It was kind of a cool day; we were wearing jackets, but it wasn't cold enough to be inside. It was mid-autumn, and the leaves had fallen, so there were leaves all over the place. We were just kinda out playing, looking for crawdads, turning over rocks, and things like that. And then we come up into the yard, and Ernen says, "Look! There's a cat! There's kitties!" I looked over and there was a cat going up the hill. Then I looked up above it going up the hill behind the canning house, and there was another kitten in front of it. Well, I thought the kitten was the mother cat, because that's how big the kitten was. Then I looked farther up the hill, and there was the mother cat. Now, the mother cat was a big cat, but it was not a cougar. It wasn't a house cat—not by any means. It was not a bobcat either, because it was dark gray and solid. It was kind of a weird smoke color; it was like a gray that really blended into the hillside.

Mom heard us yelling, 'cause she was in the kitchen, and she knew enough not to get too far away 'cause we would just take off, and we were, in fact, taking off up the hill trying to catch those kittens. The mother cat was up there going "R-W-A-A-A-A-A-A-A-A-A R-W-A-A-A-A-A-A-A-A-A," making threatening noises, and the kittens were just standing there like they wanted to come back down to us, 'cause they were curious. Then Mom comes out and saw what we were doing and saw the cat up on the hill and started screaming, "get your a——es back in the house right now!" Mom would get going, and she was loud, and her voice would echo up and down the holler.

I never saw that big cat again. However, in the summer when you'd have those lovely summer rainstorms with all the thunder and the lightning, we'd have dinner and then we'd go outside and turn off the lights in the house and sit on the porch. We would just sit outside and watch the storm for a few minutes in the dark. I don't know if anybody still does that or not. Anyway, there were some nights we would do that, and it would be before the storm would start that across the creek, straight across from the porch, you could hear things moving through the woods. You could never see it—it happened sometimes in the very daylight, too. I would look right at where I would hear it, and you couldn't see it. Whatever was moving, you could not see it, but I could hear it just fine. When you grow up in the woods like that—smack dab in the middle of the Daniel Boone Forest, and that's your backyard, you get attuned to things. Like, okay, that noise must be one of these, ya know? You figure these sounds out. But whatever it was out there moving, it was big, and I could never see it. That happened all the time.

THE HELLACIOUS BEAST OF WILD DOG ROAD

Told by Candi Sizemore Crawford

I wish I could tell you this story in a more folkloric way; it's kind of like a wild joke in our area, but a bizarre one. My paternal bloodline has lived in Hollins Fork for generations. For those of you not familiar with the area, Wild Dog Road and Hollins Fork Road are two forks off of a road up in the Big Creek area of Leslie County near the Clay County line. Anyway, I haven't seen this haint, or this beast—I always imagined it to be a beast—but I've heard stories about it from the family for many years. The last time I remember anyone mentioning seeing it was in the '90s.

The stories usually began with one of my family members trying to make it home before dark on ATVs, roaring through the hills. Those roads have a lot of rough ruts and briar bushes, and when it rains there, it really storms. They said that sometimes when they would pass by a certain hill at the edge of dark, they would feel something weird following right behind them. Now, you may have heard a lot of stories in these parts about invisible creatures on the backs of horses, or invisible haints following people so closely that you could hear the footsteps of something, or feel something behind you, but this was a little different. My family members who had encountered this said they would look back and there would be a large black figure chasing after them with glaring, animalistic eyes—that may have been why we started calling it a beast. They also said that they could feel this thing and its "glares" on their heels the whole way home—this thing could run, and it was B-I-G. They said it was "throwing up more gravel behind it" than the ATV. They would have to gun the gas to get home.

The older folks in my family would talk about this too. My papaw spoke of hearing and seeing things in the hills around Hollins Fork that he was raised in and lived in all of his life. Often as kids in Appalachia, during the Great Depression, his friends and family would bear the brunt of the weather to gather wood for their homes as per the instructions of their grandmother. Now, their grandmother was the last full-blooded Native American in the bloodline; she was fierce, strong, and more than a bit ornery. The boys would come racing home from gathering wood with tales of spooky sounds and sightings, and she would certainly have no word of it. She just gave them the order to get inside immediately, with a grim stare out to the hills . . .

My papaw and all of his folks, though, they still said the place was cursed with something. All his life he would say they heard strange, unearthly cries early in the morning and late at night that they couldn't really explain. They'd also find large, unusual footprints in the sand by the creek, and not belonging to a human, or deer, or canine, or bear, or any of the other common creatures you'd find in these parts—they were way too big. My family were often left speechless in explaining or describing these occurrences—the paleness of their face or their goose-bumped hair standing on end from racing home with this beast behind them said more than they could express in words. They always said they didn't think they could get away from it, so it must have really spooked them.

Boogers of Harvey Bend, Part 1
The Sasquatch of 476

Anonymous

It travels up and down through 476, between the Harveys' residence here and the Harveys' residence down around Caney that way, just between here and there, and I mean, it's supposedly traveling to other areas too. But anyhow, it's hairy, stinky, about like a bigfoot description . . . yeah, 'bout like a bigfoot. But it's unseen, and it has red eyes. It actually travels between homes and stuff down here. One of 'em actually attacked my aunt. And one of 'em attacked my cousin down around on the point down there. Before he passed away, years ago, he told us that he'd seen it and that it had red eyes. Yep, it attacked him.

"What do they call it?"

They's nothing they can call it; it's just an evil creature, whatever it is. Then you have another one that kinda screams like a woman but that's a big cat or something, and they are here, panthers . . . bobcats.

"Have you seen a panther?"

I haven't seen a panther, but I've seen bobcats. But, yeah, they are panthers down here, and they's been people who have posted photos of panthers on Facebook and stuff.

"Lord have mercy, that's scary—and that *bigfoot* thing!"

Well, it's traveling—

"Through the hills or on the road or—?"

In ye house! Now I've stayed down there around my great-grandma and -grandpa's place. Before they tore it down, I lived down in that place back around about 2005, after I got divorced. And yeah, there is evil down there. One night something hit the kitchen floor of my house like a big book slammed down on the kitchen floor or something. I looked in there and there was nothing there; now that's my own personal experience.

"And they don't have any explanation?"

It's always been around there; even our great-grandpas and all them knows it's there.

"And what's that area called, Hardshell?"

Hardshell—all the way down to Caney there.

"Lord, so we got us some kind of evil creature in Hardshell!"

Well yeah, Harvey Bend. Harvey Bend. That's that big curve down there where they're working on the flood relief now. I've got family there; that's Harvey Cemetery #1 up there. Up on the point up there, but you can't see it from here. And that's Harvey Cemetery #2 down there on the bend. On ye left, you'll see it on ye left as you go down there around that curve. Now my grandmother down there and her house, she saw something actually come out of the wall, but she never did tell us what it was. But it kinda came out right above her grandchild at the time, my cousin. But she was a god-fearing woman, she believed very faithfully. And she knew about good and evil, you know, ye got ye good and evil everywhere. You just gotta have faith, keep the faith. A lot of people don't believe, but I can tell ye there is evil and good in everything. If it can overtake ye, well it doesn't come after good people—I know that's sad, but it's true.

BOOGERS OF HARVEY BEND, PART 2
THE LADY IN WHITE

Anonymous

"Tell them about the Lady in the White Dress."

The "Lady in the White Dress"—well she wears a dress, obviously. Now my aunt Nora, she's seen her, years ago back in the '70s. We used to have a little truck camper here that sat in the back of ye truck, and it caught fire. Well, she saw the Lady in the White Dress appear, and mysteriously the fire went out. Don't know how, but it went out—the fire that was in the camper.

Now, in the '90s, or the early 2000s, I think it was maybe the late '90s, that whole bottom over there caught fire. And some family was sitting on my aunt's porch—two of my aunts and uncles, one was in a wheelchair, they was just porch-sitting over there across the road. And they saw that Lady in the White Dress come up, and she stood right there on the edge of that bank—right where that vehicle is over there on that bank. She stood there, and they was worried about the fire in the bottom catching the store here on fire, and lo and behold, wuddn't long after the Lady in the White Dress appeared and the fire went out. Whoever the Lady is, I guess she's like a guardian around here. And you know, anything involving a fire here, it goes out when she appears. I can't explain it rationally.

"So, you all have a guardian and red-eyed creature?"

My aunt one time, she had a medium come over here, from church, and he said, "Yeah, they's evil here." But they's also good. It's like yin and yang. Good versus evil. It's about like that everywhere ya go; you know there is good and bad in everything. But the Lady in White, she's appeared numerous times, probably many that we didn't know of, but she's appeared two or three times that I've actually saw her, we've actually saw her. I saw her up there in the yard that time when the camper caught fire. And several of them up there on the front porch saw her over here.

Just who is that Lady in the White Dress? We don't know who she is. The only one that I could say if she was a family member would be our great-grandmother that's buried up there on the hill. Up there on the point. Now, I think she was killed back in the 1930s. The old store used to be right here, and the story goes that she was in the store here late at night and someone just came in here and killed her—shot her. Pretty much right here. And we don't know who it was, how it happened, or why it happened. But, if you want my guess as to who the White Lady would be, if that was a family member's spirit, it would probably be Great-Grandma.

"Cornhusk"

Told by Miryam Jackson

The most significant personal experience I've had regarding otherworldly phenomena occurred in Alumni Woods at Berea College late one night in June or July. If you followed the trailhead beginning from Alumni Field behind the College Post Office, you would come to a split in the walking path. The main trail would eventually lead you to the upper trails that moved into the hills. The smaller side trail veered to one side, cutting through an open grassy field for two hundred yards or so before leading back into the woods on the cinder loop, which was a flat section of trail paved with post-use coal cinders. Following the cinder-loop trail one way would lead back to the main trail.

Following this trail in the other direction would lead out of the woods and past a tiny private cemetery. The first story is one I have not personally witnessed, but multiple alumni told me that there is supposedly a spectral old woman who appears late at night near the cemetery. Most sources agreed that she was generally a benign-feeling apparition, although everyone I spoke to agreed that the temperature always dropped dramatically preceding her appearance.

In either June or July 2012, a group of my friends and I were determined to go ghost hunting out in Alumni Woods. We waited until after the sun had set, banking on the general haunted reputation the woods had at night. There were about five of us altogether that set out from the post office field trailhead. When we crossed the creek bridge and got on the trail proper, our enthusiasm dimmed a little. We still pressed on.

The longer we walked, the more my nerves frayed. Every warning bell in my body was sounding off and telling me to turn around and get right off that trail immediately. Now, truthfully, I had never explored the woods late at night, because I got that same malevolent, unwelcoming feeling every time the sun dipped a bit too far behind the trees. Normally I listened to my gut; this time I ignored it.

When we came to the split in the trail, the feeling became too much for me. I separated from the group and told them I was going to wait in the tall grass clearing and get out of the woods proper for a moment and see if the bad feeling subsided. My friends quickly agreed to meet back up with me on the other side of the bridge if I chose not to rejoin them. They left me at the split and followed the main trail. I turned and followed the side trail to the prairie clearing.

When I stepped out on the mowed strip that swiped through the tangle of tall grasses, ironweed, and boneset, I waited for a feeling of relief that never came. The overwhelming feeling of heaviness and fear lifted slightly, leaving what seemed like an unnatural stillness. I remember thinking it felt like the air itself was holding a breath.

I inched further into the grass, wanting to put space between myself and the trail I had vacated. I don't remember what turned my attention, but when I was a little less than halfway between the two trail points, I looked toward the far point that led to the cemetery and cinder loop. My feet seemed to just sort of stop on their own. I found myself fixed in place, staring at that black space between the trees, holding my breath and unable to tear my gaze away. I think altogether I must have stood there only a minute or so when I saw the thing appear.

It looked at first as though a small child was standing in the entrance. I realized I had never actually felt fear, not real fear, before that moment. Its head was round, I could see. That was all I really marked, beyond its size. And then it was suddenly closer; I still don't know how—this thing didn't walk, or float, or run. It didn't move at all. But it kept growing clearer and closer. When it was on the trail, I saw that it looked as though it were made of dried cornhusk. It had a very human shape. And then I saw that it had no face.

As soon as I made out that its features were blank, I knew somehow that I was in danger. I truly can't explain this, but somehow, I knew that it "saw" me back. This outpouring of rage, hatred, and pure malevolence washed over me from the cornhusk doll. I tried to force my legs to move, but my body locked in place. I tried to scream for my friends, but I couldn't even get my mouth to open. My vocal cords may as well have belonged to someone else.

The doll was rushing motionlessly for me when I heard a clamor behind me and my friends spilled into the grass track. Everything released all at once; the doll disappeared like it had never been there. With one of my stronger friends keeping an arm around my shoulder, we all but bolted out of the woods. In the aftermath, I got from my friends that other than a growing sense of warning, they had encountered nothing.

I asked how they knew where I was, and I received odd looks in response.

"We heard you scream. We all did!"

The only screaming I had been capable of was entirely in my head. I never found anything other than guesses of what was in the woods or why it wanted to hurt me. And I never went back in the woods after sunset again.

"Big Redeye"

Told by Destiny Kaplan. This story is dedicated to the memory of her grandfather Levi Lewis.

This is a story my Papaw told me years ago. He lived up on Owl's Nest in Leslie County his entire life, right at the top of the mountain past the old log cabin. Here's how he told it to me:

> When I was in my teens, my older brother and I decided to go fishing. We chose to do an overnight fishing trip at the pond up on the tippy top of Owl's Nest Mountain, out in the back of the holler just as you're getting ready to head back down the back side of the mountain on what we called the back way, that eventually leads to the Dry Hill–MacIntosh Road, which you could take to get to Hal Rogers Parkway heading toward Hazard. It was a flat area at the very top of the mountain, deep in the sea of trees that covers that area.
>
> At about seven o'clock in the evening, we walked around the mountain and out to the area we wanted to set up our camp, set ourselves up real nice by the pond, and got started with fishing. The night was peaceful. We weren't catching much, but we were enjoying each other's company nonetheless. Everything was peaceful that night—right up until about three o'clock the next morning.
>
> At first, it was subtle. The clock hit 3:00 a.m., and I began to hearing a cracking in the trees. My first thought was that there was a bear or a mountain lion, or perhaps even a black panther, that was stalking up on us. My brother had decided to take a nap during this time. I got my gun and woke up my brother. The sounds were getting louder, closer.

I stood up and began to wait for whatever was creeping up on us to make its appearance. That was when the loudest crack I have ever heard rang out around me, like a large branch being snapped right off of the tree—and staring at me from deep in the trees was a singular, big, red eye! It was glaring, a brilliant, bright red color with a black pupil, and the being itself stood up on two feet like a human and was hairy all over.

On instinct, I fired several shots at this thing, but it was like it wasn't even fazed. More snapping and cracking in the trees and I hastened to waking up my brother because we needed to leave immediately. Now, he didn't believe me at first. It wasn't until I told him the second time, "There's something watching us!" that he believed me. We took off running, fishing poles and lanterns left where they were.

Snap!
Crack!
Crunch!

That thing was trying to follow us, and it was massive. We sped off, my brother running ahead of me, and I kept urging him to go faster. That thing began to run, chasing us but staying in the trees. You could hear tree branches just snapping off the trees, and you could see that big, red eye just trailing us. I continued to fire shots at it, but nothing came from them.

I don't know what it was or what its intent was, but I knew that whatever it was wasn't any good. It wasn't until we were almost home that it stopped following us and came no farther. We went back the next day to get the stuff that we had left, and you could see the damage that whatever that big, red eye was had done in its movements. Branches were down along the woodwork.* To this day, I don't know what it was.

Grandpa said he never did see it again, and he told me several other stories through the years about Owl's Nest, but this is the

---

*Woodwork is a colloquial term for the timberline.

one that's most prominent to me because he actually took me to the area that it happened. The area where it happened is said to have been a hanging place for Confederate soldiers during the Civil War. I don't know if there's a connection, but I do wonder if Big Redeye is still roaming around up there . . .

The Fourseam "Thing"

Anonymous

I have a story that happened back in 2016. I was just riding my four-wheeler through Fourseam late one evening. It was a perfectly normal ride until I turned to head home because it got real dark. For some reason, something didn't feel right, but I just shrugged it off and kept going. I heard gravel getting knocked up behind me, but I ignored it at first, thinking it was just my four-wheeler.

Then I noticed the sound of the gravel thrown behind me getting louder and started hearing what sounded like panting. I looked back and saw this silhouette chasing me. It was running on all fours, but it was way too big to be a bear. I laid my thumb to the gas and mashed it flat and sped back onto Poll's Creek Road, where I went in from—and sped home as fast as I could. After six years, I still have the image of this giant thing speeding toward me etched into my mind. Even now, I still refuse to ride through Fourseam by myself anymore.

The Phantom Beast of Cow Creek

Told by Sharon Gibson McIntosh. This story serves as a prelude to "Yoo-Hoo, Mary Jane!"

We've all heard yarns about spirits and beings not of this world, tales about strange happenings. The internet is crowded with photos and stories about presumed supernatural creatures, investigations, and such. But do we actually believe them? Some people say they do, while others are more skeptical. I was never in my life a believer in things like that, but in recent years, I have had to seriously modify my way of thinking.

When I was a child, my family would come home from wherever we were living at the time to Cow Creek in Owsley County, Kentucky, to visit my father's parents, Louis and Lizzie Gibson. They lived in a big old white house away across the creek bottoms from the road. I remember having a good time playing with my cousins in the yard, barn, orchard, and on the hills designated as Sheep's Hill and Cow's Hill. The grown-ups would sit around the fire at night, talking until bedtime. A subject that would occasionally be discussed was something or other which had happened over in the "hainted holler." It was a deep, dark recess that began at the gravel road and then meandered quite a ways up the hill. Stories were told about the unearthly sounds that at times could be heard coming from that mysterious place. I didn't usually stay around to hear many details of those scary happenings, because I knew I wouldn't sleep that night if I did. But it was evident that the adults believed something really bad had happened there sometime in the past, and that some "thing" or being was still mourning because of it.

As I grew up, that story gradually faded from my memory, but I remembered it shortly after my marriage, when my husband

and I went for a weekend visit to his parents' house. Someone had recently told them about hearing the sound of a baby crying in a hollow up the creek from their home. Everyone there that night revealed that they at one time or another had heard the awful sound, even Earl, my husband. They all agreed that it wasn't a noise caused by the wind or by a tree limb grating against another or even by an animal—it was definitely a baby's strange but feeble cry, and there were no words to describe the dreadfulness of it. Then someone mentioned an old house on up the hollow where the front door would never stay closed. It had been locked, barred, and even nailed shut, but always, inexplicably, it opened right back up again.

At first, I thought that those stories were being told to frighten me—to possibly make me afraid to spend the night, but I soon realized that every tale was told with complete sincerity and honesty, and I wasn't too sure that I wanted to stay there any longer, certainly not all night. And then, of all things, that quiet, steadfast man I had married told something that I had never heard before and would surely never forget—every time I think of it my hair still stands on end.

He said that one night when he was a teenager, he and a bunch of friends were going to a party, walking down the gravel road on Cow Creek—several of them, moving along in a group. They were walking slowly because Jeff, another friend, had promised to go with them and had run back to his family's home to get something that he'd forgotten. He told them to go on and he would catch up. It had become dark with just a sliver of moon to guide them, when, at last, they heard the sound of Jeff's approaching footsteps, hurrying down the road behind them.

Being the mischievous boys they were, someone suggested linking arms and forming a line across the dark road to catch the unsuspecting Jeff when he should overtake them. Quickly, they carried out their plan, locked elbows, formed their row, and waited silently to spring the surprise. The sound of footsteps on gravel was growing louder, and the boys chuckled quietly . . . waiting.

They soon began to realize that something was not right about the noise they were hearing. The footsteps were too loud—more forceful than a young man running could ever make. Then someone whispered hoarsely: "Boys, that can't be Jeff—that's got to be a horse." A large shadow was rapidly approaching, and their eyes grew wide with fright, for the thing, whatever it was—certainly not Jeff—quickly launched itself right at them and then through the row of waiting young men and hurtled on down the road. No one had felt it, and no one had touched it. It had traveled through their barricade just like the shadow that it was and clattered on its way, scattering gravel as it went.

Scary? Weird? Unbelievable? It surely was not an experience for the faint of heart. Earl and everyone present that night swear that it happened just as it is described here. When Jeff finally arrived late to the party, Earl said they told him what had happened to them on the road, but he had seen and heard nothing and was as mystified as the rest of them. What was it? No one will ever know, but they were, and still are, absolutely certain that it was not a living creature. Some may laugh at or ridicule such a story, but not me!! Absolutely not me. Not now, anyway!!

The Lurker in the Cave

Anonymous

This story is going to sound a bit more like a sci-fi movie than straight-up horror or a traditional haint tale, but nevertheless, it is my wildest encounter with a booger in these hills. Oh, and before I continue, I want to add that when you hear this story, you may think that I surely must have been smoking some good weed or had a little too much to drink on that day, but in fact I was sober and actually I am one of the most sober people you'll ever meet. So there ye go!

Back when I was a teenager, several years ago, a group of us were riding around in a car in the summertime. We were looking for an adventure, as teenagers tend to do, and we were following another carload of teenagers to see what kind of shenanigans we would all get into. We were either in Laurel County or Rockcastle County, not far from Exit 49 in Livingston, when we pulled off of the road, parked our cars, and started walking down to what the others told us was a sort of secret cavern. I wanted to say I heard a river running below, which makes sense if we were in Rockcastle County, but it could have even been East Bernstadt, which would have been even scarier.

Anyhow, you wouldn't know the place was a cave just by looking at it. It had greenery all around it, and it looked just like the hillside of a mountain. It wasn't an easy place to get to; you climb down on rocks from one ledge to another, straight down. The place honestly gave me murder-central vibes. I got the creeps thinking about what all may have taken place there. But the other group of teens knew exactly where the opening was, and we followed them on inside.

The inside of this place was quite large, and the opening was huge and cavernous. We were able to all easily fit in there and spread out several feet. Everyone could still see each other, because the opening was so large, so we started to check things out. We explored a bit, chatting, without going too far away from each other.

Me and a friend of mine, Samantha, or Sam, were about six feet away from the rest of the group, but still in the same general area. Suddenly I heard a high-pitched screeching noise. Before I had time to be scared, I saw a shadowy, fuzzy black form, at least about four feet wide, and on at least four legs, dart past us at an unbelievable speed.

Sam saw it too, because we both shrieked in horror at the site of that thing, which had again vanished from our vision by the time we had time to catch our breath again. Sam and I looked at each other in shock and disbelief.

"Did you see that?" I asked her.

"Yeah, what the hell was that?" Sam replied.

By this time, the others were laughing at us. They thought we were crazy, poking jokes, asking what we were so scared of, why we were screaming. Strangely, no one else had seen anything. Sam and I, though, were properly freaked out. Our hearts were pounding, and we begged the others to leave. We were ready to get our tails out of there.

After leaving the cave—which wasn't easy, as I'm so short I had to crawl out—I reflected upon this experience with Sam. It's a bit difficult to explain what we saw. The most rational explanation we could come up with was that it might've been a small bear cub just speeding by quickly in the dimly lit cave, but I have never seen a bear move that fast.

Sam and I both agreed that it gave us giant tarantula vibes—it was certainly hard to see, but it was at least on four legs and it was huge and fast. It was at least four feet wide and twice as big as the biggest of us there. The screeching sound we heard before we saw it made a larger impact on Sam than on me. I do remember, vaguely, hearing the screech, but I was more terrified by the sight of this thing. Sam was way more spooked by the noise. She might not have caught as good of an image of it as I did. It wasn't easy to see—we both acknowledged that we couldn't make out all of the details—but we both heard and saw something lurking in the shadows of that cave, darting out of sight so quickly we could only catch a brief glimpse of its grisly form. It was gone by the time we shouted, and that was probably for the better.

We were first in line to get out of there, and I haven't been back since. As far as I know, Sam hasn't either. I don't know exactly if I could locate it, but I do remember the general area. I'm more hefty than I used to be, so I'm not entirely sure I could still get by all those little crooks these days. But the more I think about that cave, the more it creeps me out to think about what must have happened there and what may have lived there, or what still may live there.

III   STAINED EARTH

Stained Earth—*Noun* An Appalachian Dialectical English term used to refer to a location deemed evil, haunted, or otherwise cursed.

"I Know There Are Spirits There"

Told by Rosa Couch

Now, I'm a sixty-two-year-old woman from Perry County, the Saul and Leatherwood area specifically. It's way back in the mountains, and there's some crazy stuff that goes on out here. Some of it still scares me . . .

I was born and raised here, and Graveyard Point and what we call Old Weed are two places I won't go at night. These places are down by Buckhorn Lake and the Leatherwood Recreational area—a lot of stuff goes on down there. My dad had all kinds of experiences down there night fishing, so much so that he finally quit fishing at night—said he was imposing on the spirits. My dad was a Christian and a very godly man; he spoke the truth and always told me not to go to Graveyard Point, because there was a lot of lost spirits there. Between us, we've both got several stories.

Graveyard Point is called Graveyard Point because it used to be the site of a really old graveyard. When the Corps of Engineers built the Buckhorn Dam, they moved a bunch of those old graves from there about two miles up the road to the Government Cemetery up Spruce Pine on Kentucky Highway 2022 (mind you, not the Luce-Angel Graveyard up Squabble Creek, but that ain't a place to go either). This was when they got ready to flood Bowling Town to make Buckhorn Lake. They moved those graves in the '60s, and my grandpa, the Reverend John Woods, was one of the ones that helped to move them. Grandpa told me that one of the graves they moved was of a lady who was buried in 1903 and that her skeleton had a head full of long, red hair. He was amazed at how well her hair was preserved, and he told me that because I'm redheaded mine might do that too! The bodies at Graveyard Point were buried in wooden boxes with no vaults, so it was extremely hard to get all their body parts out of the graves. He always told me, 'til right up before he passed away, that they didn't get all of them, which might explain a few things.

As I was saying, my dad used to go night fishing down there. One night, Dad was deadline fishing with his back turned to Graveyard Point, completely alone, when all of a sudden, he heard a voice from behind him: "You doing any good?" Now Dad was a little startled, because he knew he was all alone down there, but he turned around and said he saw an old man in a trench coat and a big, black, rimmed top hat standing behind him. "Nah, they ain't biting too good today, it's kinda slow," Dad replied. Suddenly he felt a tug on his line and turned back around. "Looks like I might get one after all!" Dad said. Soon the line went limp. "Well, I guess it just ain't my night," Dad said as he turned around to give his attention to the mysterious stranger. However, when he turned back around to face his unexpected company, the old man in the trench coat and the top hat had vanished into thin air. Dad said that this happened three or four times before he realized that these night visitors were spirits, but that they looked so real he thought they were living, and he could describe each encounter in detail. He said it always happened the same way: He'd be sitting at Graveyard Point night fishing, when all of a sudden, he'd hear a voice from behind him come and say hello, ask if he's catching anything, or make general friendly conversation. Then, Dad would refocus on his rod, and when he'd look back, the person he'd been speaking to was gone. He remembered every detail, down to physical descriptions and the conversations they had and the clothing they wore. He said he saw one of them wearing bib overalls and a plaid shirt. Another he remembered having a huge beard and was smoking a pipe. These haints were very humanlike, always very friendly, and always sounded and looked so "real." The last encounter he had with one of them, he said the haint visitor looked extremely familiar, so he asked him where he was from. "I'm from here," the haint said and then vanished into oblivion when Dad had the chance to look back around at him after checking his rod. That was his last night-fishing trip at Graveyard Point.

Those were my dad's tales, but I've got a few that happened to me personally. Way back in the day when we were courtin', me and my boyfriend, now my late husband, went to a dead-end road out there around Graveyard Point and parked. It was pitch-black dark. We made sure no one was there. We was just talking and listening to music and being teenagers. After we had been there for about half an hour, all at once in an instant, the whole place suddenly lit up brighter than the sun. It was everywhere! We couldn't tell where the light was coming from! Also, there was no sound! No noise like you'd hear from an engine or an airplane or nothing . . . it was very quiet there. The brightest white light I've ever seen. It almost hurt your eyes, it was so bright. And it was everywhere, from the bottom of the highway on both sides and up into the trees. It scared us to death. We started up the car and took off in a hurry—it was so scary, you couldn't hardly see to drive because of the lights—but we got out of there fast. I looked back as we were leaving, and the light had just gone out—it was total darkness again. We heard no sounds at all, just that light . . . I've never seen it again. That was thirty years ago, but I will never forget it. I have never in my life seen light like that.

There's also a place in the holler above where I live, called Mudlick, and there's a spot in that holler that everybody here flies through at night and will not stop for nothin'. We all know it as the Weed place, and all kinds of crazy stuff has happened there for years. Just about everyone who lives in Saul has had some kind of experience up there. I was driving down the road one night just above the lake, and I come upon a guy standing in the middle of the road. I slammed on my brakes and stopped just short of hitting him. He had completely disappeared, so I thought he fell and was laying there on the highway in front of my car. I jumped out to check on him, and there was nobody there. Needless to say, I flew outta there.

Another time, a cousin of mine from up in Michigan came down to visit. I had told him about the spirits down there at the lake, and he didn't believe me—told me he wanted to go down there and see them for himself. One night, a whole carload of us went down there with him. As soon as we passed Graveyard Point, my cousin started having a bad panic attack. He completely freaked out and started looking like he was having a seizure. "Get me outta here! Get me outta here! There's something here that ain't right!" he kept shouting over and over. He started crying, and kept saying he saw "people" everywhere. It spooked him bad. To this day, he won't talk about it and said he'd die before he would go back down there to Graveyard Point again.

Now I have never had anything like that happen to me or anyone else, but that place does do weird stuff to me. I get chills and shake and lose my voice and can't speak at all when I go down there at night—when I do go down there, I feel like there's people everywhere watching me. I will not go to the lake alone at night. If I do go, I go with people, and I'd never get out of the car. I know there are spirits there . . .

Tales from Bonnyman Coal Camp

Told by Mike Overbee

Okay, so my first story—Mamaw Mildred, who would be your great-great-grandmother, had a brother who was killed on a railroad track; the train ran over him in such a way that he lost his head! This happened when she was a little girl. In the coal camp, they had a gym, a Y, as they called it; a company store; and a doctor's office. In other words, all them big shenanigans happened in one particular spot in the camp. Anyhow, Mildred would go down there on Saturdays for the matinee at the theater, and on her way home, she would walk along the railroad track. Every Saturday, as she walked back home, there was a man who she'd usually find walking back in front of her—it was the headless man! Except, I guess, somehow, in death, he, or his spirit, had managed to get his head back! She'd follow him down the tracks until they'd reach a certain rock, and that man would just jolt behind that rock and just disappear!—until, of course, the next time she walked back home up that railroad track.

Now, for my next story. Your great-great-great-grandmother Suzy Campbell, who was Mildred's mother, she had three children who died of what they called "the bloody flux." Now, I've tried to research that, and it's some type of a disease that's common today, but they have a cure for it now. Basically, it caused the babies to poop themselves to death. But, anyways, she was sitting in her living room and heard a bawl, like a baby bawling, start howling from the window. This bawling noise just rolled all the way around that room to all four corners and stopped at that window. And it did that three times. She had three children, very small, who died of the bloody flux. She didn't tell the people where to put the coffins, but they put the coffins in front of that window every time. Now, you tell me what that means!

Stained Earth

And here's my last story. Talbert Holiday, Gracy Strong's father, was a sheriff of Perry County, and he had a parrot. Every morning, Talbert would get up, eat his breakfast, put his hat on, strap his guns on—he had two six-shooters—and walk out the door. The parrot completely ignored him. This happened every single morning. One morning, he got up, ate his breakfast, put his hat on, strapped his guns on, and started out the door. The parrot said, "Goodbye, Talbert!" He took his guns off and stayed at home that day!

The Restless Spirits of Beech Fork Elementary School

Told by Samantha North

When I was a kid, my mom was the preschool teacher at Beech Fork Elementary School. That meant that she had to work kind of different hours than the other teachers, because the preschool was on a little bit of a different schedule, so they would start a little bit later in the school year and they would have to stay later. So, I spent a lot of time in Beech Fork Elementary by myself, when there wasn't hardly anyone else around but the preschool teachers and their classroom. I got to do a l-o-t of exploring, on my own and also with the other preschool teachers' kids. We got into all sorts of shenanigans.

To preface this: Beech Fork Elementary is a super-duper small school. The campus is right next to the church, Upper Beech Fork United Methodist, and it's essentially one hallway. There's one hallway with the kindergarten at one end of the hallway by the front office, and then you go all the way down—first, second, third, and right before the fourth grade room was the preschool room. Then you had fourth, fifth, sixth, the art room, the storage room, the computer lab, and the library. So, the library was all the way at the end of the hallway on the right-hand side, beside the door that went out into the track and the softball field. On the other side of the school, when you enter in the front door and turn right, you hit the front office and then the big hallway that leads to all the classrooms. Well, if you turned left, there was the cafeteria, and if you went straight, there was a little hallway that had the vending machines and eventually led out to the gym.

So we explored the school a lot while we were down there during the summers, and there were several instances that I can think of where we found some spooky things. When we would be down there running around, we always heard the different legends of the things that were supposedly haunting the school. Ms. Cynthia, who was the secretary, had told us some things that she had heard while she was working down there during the summer, things about the showers in the girls' locker room turning on, and just . . . hearing things.

A very well-known Beech Fork haint was the little girl in yellow. Her legend was that once there was a little girl who loved to read and loved the library, and she would just be constantly walking around the school with a book in her hand. As the story goes, one day, she was on the bus on the way home. When she got off the bus, she stepped out in front of a car, which hit her, and, tragically, she was killed. Everybody at the school would say that she would still walk the halls of the school and merrily skip up and down the corridor. She was said to always be wearing a little yellow dress, and she would always be skipping, holding a book, and anytime anyone would ask her where she was going, she would always say, "To the li-i-brary! To the li-i-brary!" There were several teachers who said that they had seen her, and that she didn't seem like a ghost, she seemed like—just another student, but a student that they didn't recognize until they put it together that she was the girl from the legend. I can say that I never saw her, but now, I'll move on to some of the things that I did actually see while I was down there.

One night, the school had a Christmas party for all the preschool students. I got to be there because my mom was working, and I had brought a friend home with me, so she was there too. We were in fifth grade at the time, and we were far too cool for these preschoolers, ya know? We had no interest in going to the party, so we decided we were just going to roam around the school. We also had two little boys with us, our age; one of them was the son of one of the other preschool teachers, and then the other one, well I truly do not know why he was there,

I guess he was there with the other boy. But you know, we were walking around the hallway, being flirty, running amok, and we had turned all the lights off and we were daring each other to run down to the end of the hall beside the library and run back. Well, every time we would do that, we would laugh and we'd giggle. We got to the point where we were standing about twenty feet from the end of the hallway. There was a little column there that kind of separated that part of the school from the end, where the library was, and so we were standing there and daring one of the boys to go touch it. Well, we looked, and there at the end of the hallway, we could see what looked like somebody who was kind of hunched over, like they were bending down, kind of peeking out of the window, barely peeking out of it. And we were confused—we thought that it had to have been one of the kids from the party. So we just kind of stood there and stared at it. All of a sudden it turned, really quickly, and stood up, and it was huge, way bigger than a kid, and we couldn't see its face, or its eyes. We could just see that it was really, really big, and we panicked, we ran—sprinted all the way down to the end of the hallway back to the cafeteria. And we told our moms, there is something in here in this school, because it resembled a human, but it also kinda didn't, ya know? So, the teachers, they went and they walked all the way down to the end of the hallway, and they didn't see anything, and the door, the back door that goes back out to the track, had a chain on it. So, there was no way that this thing could have gotten out and left. That was my first experience.

Another time, me and one of the same boys decided that we would go and provoke the ghost that lived in the locker rooms, because the two locker rooms were totally the most haunted places in the school. That was where Ms. Cynthia had said she'd seen things, so we'd go in there periodically and try to provoke the ghosts. Even John, my husband, has said before that one time he walked in there, and all of the lockers just flew open, all at the same time. People would say you'd go in there all the time and the showers would be running; there was just always activity in there. That was also where I always felt the most unease. The big thing at the end of the hallway we saw during the Christmas party was obviously terrifying, the little girl everyone always said was a sweet spirit, but whatever was in that locker room was not sweet; it was not kind; it was bad juju. So, Trent (the boy whose mom worked there) and I, we'd go in there and try to provoke it. This would have been my sixth grade year, so it would have also been a full year after the incident at the end of the library. We decided we were going to go and do the Bloody Mary thing, you know where you go and look in the mirror and say Bloody Mary, et cetera. Well, we were in there, and we were in the boys' locker room. The way it's set up, there's a hallway, and it's super-duper narrow, and there's a wall, so you run into a wall. But if you turn left, there's a big, open area where there's lockers and blue-tile floors and white walls. And then if you turn right, there's a bathroom with one single stall and a urinal on the left and a shower on the right.

Now, that shower was the creepiest thing you've ever seen. It absolutely looked like something from a horror movie from the '90s. It was all enclosed; it was really dark in there. There wasn't a light, so you could stand in the bathroom and look into the shower, like there wasn't a shower curtain or anything on it. So that's where we decided we were going to stand and do Bloody Mary. We stood there and said, "Bloody Mary" five times, and we just kinda stood there for a second and were like, "Ok! Welp! That was stupid!" We had left the lights on because we were chicken, and we had propped the door open. About the time we finished, we heard the door slam shut, and we were like, "What the heck?" and our first thought was that it was my little brother, because he was in my mom's room. So, we ran to the edge of the door and pushed it back open and saw that it wasn't Thomas (my little brother); he wasn't there. So, we kinda crept back in. We were standing in there where the bathroom met the shower, and we heard the toilet just start running, like when you flush a toilet and it runs and runs and runs.

We thought, "OK, that's a bit creepy." But then the shower started dripping, and it started, like, running. At first it was just dripping really heavily, and then it started running like it just turned on. And then the lights started to . . . I guess bounce is the best word for it. They weren't flickering on and off; it was just wobbling. We took all of that as our cue to get the frick out of there. So we ran out to the door and didn't look back. I have not been back to that locker room since that happened. We did go to stand at the door a couple of days later, because we would *not* go back in there, but we did stand at the door and whistle. I think it was Trent who just made a little whistling tune. And after a few seconds it "echoed" back to us, except it wasn't an echo, I am 100 percent sure of that. It was not an echo. It sounded like someone, or something, just whistled right back to us. It was so scary.

But yeah, those are my stories of Beech Fork. It's kind of funny too, because after the school shut down, that was the year it shut down, actually, my sixth grade year—so it kinda started falling apart. And it went downhill really quickly. Well, during college, I worked down there after it had become the senior citizen's center. I was still very, very careful about which rooms I went into. I never went into those locker rooms after that; I never felt good. That hallway at the end where the library was, I would never go back down there by myself—just because it still felt very ominous. Even driving by the school now, like it's all dark and spooky and it just feels very . . . dark and spooky. It just feels like everybody left, and left the spirits there alone to just kinda . . . take over the school.

My Haunted Double-Wide

Told by Tracy Banks Shepherd

Now, I'll tell you about what I consider to be "my" haunted house. We bought the home brand-new; it's a double-wide trailer. We moved it onto this property which has . . . quite the history. Back in the '70s, a lot of people did a lot of partying and a lot of fighting on this little piece of land, and a couple of people were shot and killed here.

It all started when we first moved here; we bought this double-wide in October 2005, brand-spanking new. After they set it up, myself, my oldest daughter, who was seven at the time, and my youngest daughter, Alicia, who was just a year old, got us a kerosene heater and a blow-up mattress, and we slept in the living room. We didn't want the place to just sit here all by itself of course. My husband stayed at our other home, because we had stuff there and didn't want it to get stolen or anything. There was no electricity or anything in this double-wide—as I said, it was brand new—and me and the girls were just sitting there, candles going, kerosene heater burning, and we hear a cabinet door slam. I said, "Girls, did you hear that?" My oldest said, "I did." So, I went in there with a flashlight and tried to figure out exactly where this noise had come from. The exact noise we heard is similar to when you pull open a cabinet door about five inches and it just slams back. I couldn't find anything that might have caused the sound, but this phenomenon goes on 'til this day. We've lived here since October 2005, and this is still happening now. When we have company, and company will hear it, we just say, "That's our ghost!" jokingly, but we've never seen it with our own eyes. We have all heard it though. And from that, it's progressed to the refrigerator opening, and again we don't see it, but always hear it. When you have a refrigerator opening, you know, it makes the distinct sound of the seal coming open, and then you'll hear it close back—so, that's how our haunting started: the cabinet door began making that noise.

As time goes by, other little things started happening. My sister was babysitting one night—my girls are in bed and she's sitting in the living room. Suddenly, she hears a noise from the kitchen and goes into the kitchen to investigate. One of the chairs at the dining room table had scooted sideways. This incident scared her so bad she wouldn't even stay here with my kids anymore for the longest time.

Now, there was a big, long wall that ran from my living room to the hallway, and then you make a left and there's the guest bathroom, and the girls' bathrooms are on each side. Alicia, my youngest, was about three at the time, and she hadn't been in her toddler bed for too long and we were still working on that. That night, I had put her in her bed four or five times, I reckon, and she still kept getting up. That night, I was setting right where that big, long wall ends and connects to the living room; we had a rocking recliner setting there. I was just getting settled in for the evening to watch me something on TV and have a cold Pepsi. Well, all of a sudden, I hear pitter-patter coming down the hallway, through the kitchen, I mean, and I said, "ALRIGHTY, YOU ARE GONNA GET YOUR BEHIND BUSTED!" I look up and around, and there is nothing there. I get up, go into her room, and she's actually fast asleep! I don't know what happened in that case either, but that one always freaked me out.

Another night, we were sitting here on the couch, and from a certain angle on our sectional, you can kind of see straight into our master bedroom. We almost always keep the door open to our master bedroom. I was sitting there, and I see this, almost like an apparition walk past the door from my side of the bed to the closet—which leads to nowhere, I mean. I'm sitting there cross-legged on the couch in the living room, and I'm wondering if what I'm seeing is really what I am seeing. All of a sudden, this apparition, which was made like a thin woman, turns to look at me, and her face is scrambled—like a fuzzy channel on a TV, scrambled. It wasn't no time after that, I got a phone call saying my stepmom had been put on life support, and I distinctly remember when I first saw that apparition, that was exactly who came to mind—my stepmom. So that was another unexplained event.

Another time, I was sitting on my porch swing one summer evening, and from my porch swing you can see through my screen door through the living room into the dining room. This is the entrance that most people use to come into and out of our house. My kids said they were going to Mamaw's house, meaning my mother's, who lived just a few minutes up the road. I was just setting on the porch swing, and the kids are raring to go, so I said, "Oh yeah! Hammer down! Go on!" I had my niece and nephew with me that day, as well as my own kids. My youngest daughter was probably twelve or thirteen at the time, and my oldest daughter was in her upper teens—and she's got long blonde hair. I thought they had all left and that they'd been gone a few minutes, when all of a sudden, I see that big, long blonde head of hair turn around and I hear the door slam and see her go out the back door. I said to myself, "I thought they were gone?"—because I thought they'd been gone a few minutes. I get up and look around, and I'm wondering what in the world is going on, because the vehicle they left in is gone. I was so confused. When they came back, I said, "Did you come back through the door?" Like, did you forget something? Or what happened? My eldest daughter said flatly, "No, I went out before everyone else did." So apparently, we've come to the conclusion that on that particular day, I must have seen my eldest daughter's doppelganger.

There's just so many things that have happened in this double-wide personally to us. I've told you about my experiences, but even my husband has started witnessing things here, and he is not a believer in the paranormal. However, I believe he's starting to become one . . .

The Old Hyden Elementary Gym

Anonymous

Everyone I've ever heard talk about it says the old Hyden Elementary Gym is creepy. Even my granny, who was totally not superstitious at all, said she hated to be in there alone. Given the place's history, it's pretty easy to see why. Pretty much my entire family is involved in education and has been for generations, so I've heard one story or another about when various buildings were put in or taken out of commission.

First of all, the gym is located directly beside one of the oldest graveyards in Leslie County. That graveyard is perched on a small hill directly behind Central Presbyterian Church of Hyden. The oldest tombstones are monumental in stature and well-worn with age, marking the final resting places of some of the first settlers of Leslie County. That would be spooky enough, but there is a legend about the church as well. I've been told that on a certain day of the year—I don't know which one—if you walk around that church three times backward at midnight and look in one of the windows, you will see a ghostly marriage taking place. I haven't tried it out. I don't know what day of the year you're supposed to attempt this, and I don't know who the ghostly bride and groom and their wedding party are supposed to be—but it just goes to show you, the ground this gym is built on is quite old and has quite a bit of local folklore surrounding it.

More to the point, when they were putting in the old Hyden Gym, apparently, they found two Civil War–era graves and had to try and relocate them. Now, I have no clue how true that is, and for what it's worth, I've heard the same thing about the Leslie County high school as well, and again, stories like this definitely set a grim scene.

What's certainly true is that when the infamous Hurricane Mine disaster of 1970 happened, they laid the bodies out in the gym for identification. There's plenty of documentation for that, plus my papaw was there helping. Tragic events like that are what make ghost stories a lot of the time, especially when they become a scar on the town. Even if it didn't actually make the place haunted, it would be hard to not be unnerved by the place if you knew the story—and everyone here does.

If we're talking actual hauntings, I only know of two personally. Remember how I said my grandma didn't like to be in the gym alone? Well, unfortunately she had to be a lot. She taught health and PE her whole career, and her office was there with, I think, one other teacher. She said it was so quiet and creepy being the only person there, but the worst part was when she'd be the only one there, and she would know it because the door made a loud sound if anyone went in or out, and the noises started. Here she'd be working, and all of a sudden there'd be these loud, echoing footsteps pacing the gym out of nowhere. I mean literally out of nowhere. There'd be nothing there, at all. I think she was very happy when she was able to move her office.

Another story about the old Hyden Gym was told to me by a friend who went to school there. After they remodeled the gym in the early 2000s, they used to host a lot of school assemblies as well as larger community events. This meant that the day prior to these events, they would lay a large tarp on the hardwood floor and set up probably fifty to a hundred chairs on the floor in front of the stage to accommodate those who wouldn't fit on the bleachers. The gym also housed the Hazard Community and Technical College at the time, so there was a lot of offices and classrooms on the second floor. Cameras and technical recording equipment would be set up to record the goings-on on stage. Well, one of the nights before a large event, I think it was a Veterans Day ceremony or something, the brother of the person who told me this—who was hired as the cameraman for the proceedings—decided to try a little experiment. Much like every other kid who attended Hyden Elementary, he had heard the stories about the haunted gym, and he wanted to see if he could catch anything on camera if he left the recording equipment on overnight. So that's exactly what he did.

Later on, after the event was over and he had time to rewatch his additional footage, he was disappointed to see that much of the night had passed in a completely uneventful manner. That is, until right after the film had been recording for about seven hours, or right around 3:00 a.m. At this time, he heard a strange sound in the dark, completely abandoned gym. The sound, as the film revealed, was the result of a single chair in the second row being dragged, ever so slightly, diagonally to the right and out of position by a disembodied force. It remained that way for the rest of the recording.

By the time the cameraman had arrived to pick up the footage, someone had obviously repositioned the chair. One can only imagine what went through the minds of the custodial staff when they returned in the morning to find the row of chairs they had so carefully aligned the day before ever so slightly ajar.

The old Hyden Elementary Gym building is still in use as part of the Kentucky School of Bluegrass and Traditional Music, and I'm not aware of any recent reports of otherworldly happenings there. However, if you ask any student who attended Hyden Elementary while it was operational, and much of the staff who worked either at the school, for the board of education, or for the community college, you are bound to hear loads of stories of eerie knocks, shadow people, and unexplainable events occurring at the old Hyden Gym.

"Sam"

Told by Tonya Moore

My mom bought a house in East Bernstadt, in Laurel County. It was this really, really nice log cabin, and it sat right up on top of this hill. A long, huge blacktop driveway led the way up to it from the main road, and it just went up and up and up—very steep. The only house up on that hill was my mom's house. So, they moved into it, and after a bit they started hearing funky stuff. They started hearing things hitting on the inside of the walls. Cabinet doors would move by themselves, and if somebody "new" came to the house, the lights would start going on and off. Also, they had a security system, and the security system would start tripping from time to time for no apparent reason; it had these strobe lights that would start flashing at random times.

Mom would wake up in the middle of the night several times, and there would be this dark shadow standing over top of her bed. My little sister, she wouldn't even be in her nursery, and baby toys would start going off. I kid you not: toys would start walking. My little sister had this bear, in her crib, that my mom kept in her crib. And back when my sister would sleep with my mom, my mom would hear noises like people speaking in the nursery and talking, and she would get up to go and investigate. When she got to the nursery, she would find the bear laying on the floor, outside of the crib, and toys scattered all over like someone had been playing there. I mean it was just crazy the stuff that went on there, like you could just feel this thing, you know?

The attic room of that house has its own stories. I was coming down the attic stairs one time and this . . . shadow thing, *whooooooo*, oh gosh, it ran straight through me! Like, literally, I ran into it, this black shadow, oh gosh—ooof. It just ran—*pshooo*—right through me like that. *I freaked out*, and I just had to pack my things up and leave. But you could start driving up that driveway, and you'd just get this strange, eerie feeling that something was watching you out of those tiny little windows up there in the attic. It was so bad I didn't want to go in that house by myself. If other people weren't there, I wouldn't go in. I'd sit out in the car at my mom's and wait for her to get there, because that house was so creepy.

But the creepiest thing ever, well first of all, the door leading to the attic was connected to this room that was basically our storage place. We never had any problems opening that door, never. And one night we heard this noise, and so we tried to open the attic door and it would not open. I mean, it would *not* open. We tried everything, and the door wasn't moving. And you could hear something growl like this awful, awful, awful growling sound, and this door was just like, "No, you're not getting in here." So, we went and got my stepdad. He came up, and he pried the door open, and this god-awful screechy howling sound came out! But, once we got inside, there was nothing in the attic . . .

So now here's the part that's going to freak you out. The first people to live in that house, the ones who built it, they had two little boys. I'm getting goose bumps just thinking about this. And as I told you, the house was way up on this big hill. There was a big barn at the foot of the hill, and these two little boys were sleigh-riding one day in the winter. One of the little boys hit that barn going down that hill, and he died. And his name was Sam. When we found out about this, when this stuff started happening, we started calling it by name. We would say, *"Stop it, Sam!"* and everything would just stop, immediately. I swear, when we found out that that little boy's name was Sam, and we started talking to that thing and calling it by that name, it quit doing whatever it was doing. And my mom sold that house *at last* because it was so creepy, scary, you know. Haunted, I mean. I could go on and on. And literally, I mean, yeah, this was the creepiest stuff ever, and there's a reason I'm pulled over at the gas station right now talking to you over the phone instead of at home, because I will not bring this stuff into my house! Because I know what it was like at my mom's old place, and I *do* not want any of that bad juju at my house!

"A Soul Left to Wander"

Told by Haley Wells

When I was little, I attended Hyden Elementary in Leslie County, Kentucky. I remember the school always feeling off, especially the girls' bathrooms on the first and third floors. It always had an eeriness to it, and I still have nightmares about it at twenty-one years old. I remember one time a friend and I wanted to go get a snack from the cafeteria and something to drink from the machines. Well, we walked down to the first floor, straight to the cafeteria. Now, this was a big school with long corridors and hardly any windows on the first-floor hallway, so it was dim at times. And at the end of the halls there was an elevator for staff to use, but they never did.

So, we got our drinks and snacks and started making our way back to class. As we were walking down the hall and about to turn to go up the stairwell, I see a six-foot (or taller) dark figure walking down the hall, carrying a lunch pail in his right hand. It would swing back and forth, and you could just barely make out the overalls they were wearing. I honestly thought this was just a janitor or teacher walking down the hall. I kept watching to see if they would turn around, but they kept walking until they made it to the end of the long, dim hall, where the elevator was. It walked straight into the elevator doors and disappeared. I had no idea what just happened and asked my friend if she had seen it. She said no, so we just went back to class.

Later on in life, I found out that the school and gym were used to identify the bodies of the victims of the Hurricane Mine disaster of 1970. So now, as an adult, I wonder if I saw one of the miners wandering around the school, trying to find their way home.

Haunted Antebellum Property in Jackson County

Told by Candi Sizemore Crawford

Some years ago, my family purchased some property in Jackson County, Kentucky. On the property stood a couple of very old buildings, which my family would ultimately convert into homes. These buildings were constructed during the antebellum period, or, for those not familiar with this term, the period prior to the Civil War, making them well over a hundred years old. One of the buildings was an old post office; it was one story and a rather small building. The other building stood two stories high and had an attic in the top. When they began exploring the properties, the family found some old items left from the previous occupiers, such as a rocking chair left behind in the attic.

Family pictures taken in front of the old houses would show "orbs" and strange colored spots in the photos after the film was developed. Old Mamaw Mae decided to live in the big house. She was used to being alone and getting by on her own mostly. Sometimes, though, it didn't seem she was quite alone in the big house. It wasn't long after she'd moved in before doors started slamming by themselves, dishes would rattle of their own accord, and faint sounds of someone saying "Get out!" could be heard in whispered voices throughout the house. Spooky stuff, right? But that was only what happened in the big house.

Jane and Rick were the newlyweds in the family and moved into the simple one-story former post office. They weren't home much, often busy and on the go, as newlyweds tend to be. Jane used to recall how quiet the house was. Many times, however, she awoke to the sound of what she thought were her husband

Rick's footsteps clambering throughout the house. One night she awoke to the very same footsteps; he seemed to be pacing back and forth throughout the house for hours on end. However, this being a semi-regular occurrence, she thought nothing much of it. She rolled over to go back to sleep and snuggled up to . . . Rick—who was sound asleep in bed!

These are just two of the many spooky stories I've heard from my family who lived on that old property in Jackson County. I can't remember them all, but I do remember how old and creepy those buildings were. Sometimes I wonder if they are still standing.

"Evil Hanner" and the Legend of Blood Rock

Anonymous

This was a story I first heard from my grandma when I would go stay with her when I was a little girl. She had this habit of mentioning things offhand that I would later find out were part of a bigger story. One time, she mentioned one of her sisters being afraid of this one particular rock where they grew up in Bailey Branch and that she would never go back there—although she wouldn't say why. Apparently, her sister would have visions when she would sit on different rocks, and when she touched this one specific rock, she turned white as a sheet and started shaking all over. They called it Blood Rock, and she was terrified of it. Now, I was curious about this, as any child would be, so I pressed her about it. "What happened? What did your sister see?"

Finally, she got fed up and said she didn't know but thought it had something to do with the mean old woman who used to live up there. Well, that just floored me, and I had to know more. She said that a long time ago there was a mean old witch who lived up there and that she fell in love with another man. The story goes that she and her lover murdered her first husband by ambushing him in the holler and shooting him and that when neighbors finally found him, he had bled out on this big rock that stuck out from the creek. Grandma said she thought her sister had gone up to that rock and seen the bloody outline of his body, which was the tall tale in the holler. Supposedly, the rock was haunted and you could still see the outline when it got wet.

It wasn't until I was a bit older that I found out there was more to it. My family has a copy of Dan Caudill's memoirs, in which

he tells the same story. As he tells it, the evil witch-woman killed her husband with the help of her lover and then went on to kill the two small children she had from the marriage, by sticking hatpins down their soft spots. He wouldn't say the old woman's name or how she disposed of the children's bodies, but Grandma told me her name was Hanner and that she fed them to the hogs and put what little was left over in a small box. They were never able to prove anything with any of the murders, but she supposedly confessed to all this on her deathbed before going into a fit, saying her body was "on fire" and she could hear "chains rattling from hell."

There's little bits and pieces of the story that I've heard here and there over the years. Some said that Hanner's husband beat her, and that's why she killed him. Others said she was a witch who could make people sick and make them do evil for her. I even heard someone say that people who moved into her old homeplace could hear babies crying at night. There's different versions, and I recently heard that they destroyed Blood Rock because of the haunting. It seems like most people have forgotten the story now. I think the people who knew didn't want to talk about it, because whatever the truth was, it was horrible. Grandma told me once, "Truth will set you free, and it can get you killed, too." Maybe they're afraid of old Hanner even in death, because those who knew her back then seemed to think she was just that evil. I've never gone to Bailey Branch to look for the stone at Second Fork or find her grave at the old cemetery where she's supposedly buried, but I certainly believe there has to be some truth to it all.

The Spirit Drums

Told by Candi Sizemore Crawford

Growing up, we were outside all the time on the farm. My brother and I would play all over that land. One evening as the shade was coming over from the setting sun, we heard something unusual. A steady, repetitive beat of a sound that I couldn't quite place immediately.

I couldn't tell exactly where it was coming from, but it was loud and all around us, surrounding us from every direction. My heart raced—the sound was intriguing, wild, unbelievable. The sound pounded louder and louder. At the same time, it felt familiar. Then I realized: it was the sound of drums.

It had to be thousands of them. This was completely unexplainable, and there would have been nothing like the type and number of drums I was hearing echo for miles. I don't mean drums like a band practicing in a garage. I'm talking eighteenth-century Native American tribal drums. It was wild, crazy, and beautiful. My brother and I both were big-eyed and speechless, staring at each other in disbelief. What was this? And why was it happening? What would happen next? Both of us expressed some form of verbal disbelief, such as "What?!" Not that we could hear each other's voice as the drumming continued louder and felt like it was running through my blood.

After a bit, the sound came to a stop. Our mother returned from atop a hill on the farm a little later. Bewildered, we tried to explain to her and ask if she had heard them as well. She had to have heard; they were everywhere and booming as if we were encircled in an ancient celebration. She looked at us as puzzled as we must have looked to her; she was unaware of any drumming.

Brother and I again looked at each other in disbelief. We may never know for sure what this occurrence was.

I interpreted it as a sign of protection from our ancestors. As Sizemores from Leslie County, Kentucky, we have an abundance of Native American heritage, deep-rooted in the bloodline as some of the earliest people to settle here. Though it was bizarre and unbelievable, it felt familiar, and I'd like to believe it was some form of protection from unseen evils close to us.

The Wrong Side of the Law

Anonymous

There is an old cemetery known as the Morgan Family Cemetery—or the Saltwell Cemetery, near Hoskinston, in Leslie County, Kentucky, that a lifelong resident of the community, who wishes to remain anonymous, told me contains the unmarked mass grave of an entire family murdered by a US federal marshal in the bad old days of 1900. The graves in question are buried outside of the fence of the current cemetery, which my source explained as follows.

"Well, the old Saltwell Cemetery, it used to have a fence running in kind of a *T* shape, but they removed it to make room for other people. Below that fence, there are other graves that were unmarked; one of them belonged to the Strong family. They took up around here where that church stands, in what used to be the only house in that bottom. There was five of them, Bob Strong, his wife, their two children, and his brother." According to the story, "Bob Strong was more or less an outlaw, and the federal men was forevermore after him. He shot and crippled a federal man and was running from the law and had been for a year. And the federals came in one night, and they shot the house all to pieces. They splintered it. They was a whole crew of federal men, and they killed him, his brother, the woman, and two children, aged eight months and three years. All of them."

After this horrific tragedy occurred, I am told, a certain group of local men, known as the Happy Pappy crew, were called in to dig the mass grave. All of the bodies were interred in one hole and laid unceremoniously to rest without a headstone. This should have been the end of the story, but the rest of the Strong family would be disturbed yet again, when the road through Stinnett (US Highway 421) was moved and rebuilt.

"When they was first buried, they were put right there in that road, then they built the state highway and cut a road right through the mountains. It was the same Happy Pappy crew that came and helped them dig that grave; they kept digging down to about five feet, and then the men from Frankfort came and told them to stop and leave. Then they [the US marshals] moved in and took over. But now they took a high lift and cut a big trench down there over the graves and didn't move the rocks down. It was that whole Happy Pappy bunch; they were supervised by the Frankfort people, and when they got about five feet down they made them crawl out of the holes and leave. But anyhow, yeah, they went out there to that Saltwell Cemetery, took a backhoe, and dug that hole and put 'em all in it. Ever one of 'em."

It is there, somewhere on the edge of the fencing of the modern Saltwell Cemetery, that the remains of the twice-buried Strong family sleep for eternity in an unmarked grave. The location of their remains will likely remain a mystery forever.

Chaney's Knob

Told by Tonya Moore

There's a place up in the holler called Chaney's Knob. Well, the significance of Chaney's Knob is that years and years and years ago, back when my Mamaw was young, there was this woman who lived there named Chaney. She lived up there with her husband, and he had four kids. I want to say that their last name was Stacy, that she'd married a guy called Henry Stacy, but I'm not sure—anyway, he had four kids of his own. They lived up on that knob, and they had a house there.

Well, Chaney really did not like her husband's children. She was really, really mean to them, and she would beat them, regularly. She'd line them up one at a time and just mete out the beatings one by one, spreading it out. This eventually killed the children . . . all of them. She beat them to death. All four of them. And so she remained married to Henry, and eventually he died, leaving Chaney alone.

Well Chaney herself grew old, and when she was getting ready to die, you know, back in the old days they'd have people sitting up with you when you're getting ready to pass at your house. So, they were sitting up with Chaney, and my Mamaw was there, she was one of 'em. All of a sudden, Chaney started just screaming and kicking and wailing, and just screaming and going out of her head. She started screaming, "Get them off me! Get them off of me! Get these kids off of me! They are hanging on to my feet! They are hanging on to me! GET THEM OFF!" And she was just like squirming and screaming and flailing all over the bed. There were no kids there. There were no kids whatsoever. There was nobody there except the old folks staying up with her to accompany her as she passed.

And so after she died, 'til this day, when you go up there on Chaney's Knob, you can still hear kids crying and screaming. Now my mom told me this story, and apparently, you can still hear the kids screaming up there. Her mother, my Mamaw, was there when Chaney passed, and they both told me that Chaney was just screaming and railing and telling her to "Get these kids off of me! GET THESE KIDS OFF OF ME!" And I don't know if it was just her conscience or if it was, you know, something that she was really experiencing, you know like these kids pulling on her and stuff, all the lives she had taken. I don't know, but for my Mamaw to be like, you know, I was there and this is what she was doing. When my mom was telling me this, to be honest I was envisioning that scene from *The Exorcist*, you know? But yeah, apparently, to this day, you can go up there on Chaney's Knob and you can still hear those poor kiddos a-crying.

IV   HIGH STRANGENESS

High Strangeness—*Noun* Uncanny, inexplicable occurrences or observations that defy neat categorization into other types of paranormal phenomena.

Astronomer J. Allen Hynek coined this term in reference to the behavior of unidentified flying objects (UFOs) or unidentified aerial phenomena (UAPs) during the 1970s.

"A Thinness, Where Things Can Bleed Through"

Anonymous

There's a couple of things that went on that I can tell you because they personally happened to me. I don't think I ever talked to you about this, mostly 'cause I didn't want to freak you out. Now, my dreams about this sort of stuff started before I moved into that house, which is why I don't think it was so much the house as it was just the "thing" reacting to us. I lived on the absolute other side of the mountain, in an old house next to John L. and Annie's, which was like, straight up the mountain and then down on the other side. This would have been when I was about four or five years old. Mom rented it when I was three and Earnest was probably one and a half, and then she married David and had Kelly when I was five. Back then, I started having what I called "dreams," but I'm starting to think that maybe they were something else.

One night, I dreamed that it was dark. For some reason, Earnest and I were outside of the house, outside of the fence, in Annie and John L.'s driveway. We were facing the mountain that sat behind the house, kinda hunkered down behind a little car. I can still see it plain as day in my head. There was something in the shed like a little fire, but like a little demon; if you looked at it, you wouldn't say demon, per se—you would think that it was more of an imp—and Earnest and I had to get back to the house without the little demon-imp thing seeing us. Subconsciously, little me knew what that was, and I should not have, because we didn't go to church regularly and we didn't talk about stuff like that. Somehow, I just knew, which kind of freaks me out now when I think about it consciously. Earnest was scared, and I was, too, but I was more angry 'cause I knew we'd get into trouble if we didn't get back in the house. He was like, "No, we gotta stay here and hide," and I didn't even think about it. I just stood up, and it saw me and started posturing like it was gonna come and get us. I sorta planted my feet, fisted my hands, and said, "You don't belong here! You have to leave right now!" And I made it leave so we could go back.

Around the same timeframe, we moved up to the old house, and we were in those back bedrooms. In that house, we would hear music from the '30s and '40s playing in the wall where an old fireplace had been covered. It sounded like it was coming from a radio somewhere faint. I would hear it every time I would be in there reading. This happened fairly often, and it happened to different people; it wasn't just us. We'd see shadow people up there; I saw them a lot in that old house. Seeing them and hearing that old-timey music was very common. In the back end of the house, where the back end of the hill would come down and it would get really close to the back end of the house, that's where the kids' bedrooms were. That was my bedroom, and on the other side of the bathroom was Earnest's bedroom. At night, the door would be open, and the hallway light would be on, so that we could go to the bathroom. With the door open, it would cast a little sliver of shadow, and in that shadow would be that little eight- to twelve-inch-tall demon-imp thing sitting there squatted on its haunches. If you tried to look at it straight on, you couldn't see it. You had to kinda glance at it sideways. It would just be sitting in that shadow, looking at you.

It was scary when you're a little kid, and I hate to say this because I feel like it's misleading, but at the same time, I felt sad for the little creature because it was miserable. I wasn't inviting it to stay. It had to get on down the road. Ya know? "You gotta go." But I wasn't afraid of it; I was scared at first when I noticed it. I realized this thing was miserable—it's sitting there and it's just looking all washed up and pitiful. I don't know what it was. I don't know what it was about that place, that house, but for some reason... I don't know. Maybe it's just one of those places, but my theory is that it's just one of those areas where there's a thinness, where things can bleed through. There's things you don't speak of, because to speak of it brings it to your attention, and then it comes to you...

The Hairy Arm

Anonymous

I had a truck driver, I'm pretty sure his name was Kyle Bledsoe; anyhow he drove a truck for me. He'd usually get home from work about nine–ten o'clock of a night, so he'd like to have a coupla beers and sit down and watch the evening news before he went to bed. It was the summertime, and he had the TV over in the corner and the window was open. As he was sitting there watching the news on TV, this big, long, hairy arm came through the open window, reached right across, picked his TV up, pulled it through the window, cords and all loose from the wall!

He said it scared him so bad that he couldn't react to it—he couldn't run outside and see whatever was happening. It took him four–five minutes just to recover from it! That happened up on Coon Creek. Now, I don't know if it was a Sasquatch or a Bigfoot or what have you; I don't think he "measured any tracks" or anything. I think—really and truly—I think someone just stole his TV, but he did say it was a big, long, hairy arm and that it sure gave him the fright of his life. I don't know what he ended up doing about his TV, though!

"Do You See That?"

Told by Destiny Caldwell

I have seen UFOs in eastern Kentucky a couple of times. Most of the time, I saw them in Knott County and Letcher County, but sometimes I've seen them in Leslie County. Most of the time, they are just about the size of a star. It's just a small dot, but if you watch it, you can see it go all the way across the sky. Usually, you know, you can see satellites move and things like that, but these just seem to be moving a little faster—those you can see pretty often.

However, the most incredible and unbelievable time that I saw a UFO was in London, Kentucky. It was the Fourth of July, and I was in high school. I was going to a Fourth of July celebration with my boyfriend at the time and his sister, at his other sister's house in London. This was after we had watched the fireworks and everything, and he had decided to stay a few nights with his sister, so me and his other sister, Allie, decided to drive back. I think her son was also in the car, but he might have been asleep—he was pretty young at this time. He was in a car seat.

Driving back, we were just talking and just driving; we were still somewhere around London, cause we were definitely still in town. I look over and I see—a couple hundred feet in the air—a giant red ball just floating in the air unmoving. I watch it for a couple seconds. And then she eventually notices it too, and she asks me, "Do you see that?" And I'm like, "Yeah! I do see that!" So, she pulls over, and we both start watching this orb floating in the air, and we watch it for a couple minutes, and it just, ya know, isn't moving at all. It obviously isn't a firework, cause it would have dissipated already.

Eventually, it started to kind of wiggle from side to side. And we were like, "What's happening? I've never seen anything move like that. I don't understand." And then, it just shot up—just straight up into the sky and disappeared. To this day, I don't know what that was. I have no idea what it could be. I've never heard of any kind of technology that could look like that, and this was before commercial drones were even popular.

"You'd Think There'd Be Blood Somewhere"

Told by Keisha Morgan

This one my granny would tell me and Beverly as a bedtime story. Her dad, Great-grandpa Hector, went out hunting one day, and he got ran up a tree by a bunch of wild hogs. He figured he'd just set up in the tree until they got bored of him and then he could leave, but hours passed, and it seemed like the hogs were just getting madder and madder about him being in the tree. It was getting dark quick, and he wasn't about to be out in the mountains overnight—but he definitely didn't have enough of anything with him to fight off the hogs. He started yelling, and he knew it wasn't going to help anything, because there wasn't anyone around to hear him, but he yelled anyway.

To his surprise, he did see someone walking toward him, so he started hollering more. Now, he said that the guy walking toward him looked just like him. *Identical.* Down to the clothes he had on and everything. He wasn't packing no gun or anything, so Great-grandpa was yelling at this guy to go get help, because he was sure the hogs would eat him up if he came any closer. He just kept walking, though—kept walking toward the tree and the hogs. The hogs took a minute, but they finally noticed him, and they charged at him. He just stood still. Hector claimed that he heard his own voice telling him to run while he still could, so he did. He came back the next day with his brothers, and they checked out the scene for anything of the man's. He was sure that the hogs had got him, but they didn't find anything. Not even any blood. Which, I guess, isn't super weird with wild hogs, because they really will eat clothes and everything else. You'd think there'd be blood somewhere or something . . .

Being a Caul Bearer

Anonymous

From time to time, a baby will be delivered in an unbroken amniotic sac (bag of waters) or with some of the amnion (membrane) covering their face. They are said to be "born with a veil over the face" and are known as caul bearers. Such children have, for centuries, been both feared and revered. Being born behind the veil (holy hood) comes with a multitude of superstitions, and some claim such children can have supernatural visions. It is estimated that somewhere between one in one thousand and one in eighty thousand babies are born in the caul.

I was born a caul bearer. From as long as I can remember, I have always felt different and could, what I call, "feel energy." My youngest recollection of my knowing I was different was sensing that someone close to me was going to die. My grandparents and I would always visit my grandmother's mom (I called her Maw) in Molus, Kentucky, at least once or twice a week. She gave birth to twelve children, four of whom were two sets of twins. One set of twins only lived a few hours after birth, and of the other twin set, only one of the pair survived to adulthood. She raised eight small children alone after her husband was murdered.

I was very young—five years old—when I experienced my first memorable vision. My grandparents and I were leaving Maw's house after a visit, and my grandmother didn't hug her mom goodbye. Maw was standing in the porch, and my grandfather was grumpy and wanted to go home, and my grandmother kept trying to get me in the car. I could not take my eyes off Maw. I saw her as clear as day, surrounded in a brilliant white light and being "laid out" in her living room as everyone was crying. As quickly as the vision appeared was as quickly as it left—Maw was again standing on the porch and waving bye. I told my grandmother to go hug Maw goodbye, and she was resistant and wanted me to get in the car because my grandfather was grumpy and wanted to leave. I remember telling her, "No, you need to go hug her goodbye. She is going to die tonight."

I remember getting a tongue-lashing from my grandfather all the way home to Baxter, because I had made my grandmother upset: "Why would you say such horrible things?" For that, I had absolutely no answers. I didn't know why I said it or how I knew it, but I did! I knew she wasn't going to be with us anymore. Later that evening, we did get a call that Maw had passed at the age of eighty-three. A few days later, we sat up with her, and the scene in that living room in that old wood house in Molus was exactly what I had seen as we were leaving that day. Today, I still feel things, but I have never experienced anything as strong and as clear as I did on that January day in 1967.

"And I Ain't Been Back Since!"

Told by Nathan McDaniel

Well, I was working in the coal mines at Smith Coal Company when me and my wife first got married, and I had a bunch of beagle hounds. So, I worked that night, and I told my wife, "When I come in, I'm gonna take these dogs rabbit hunting in the morning." She says, "Okay, go right ahead." So, the next morning I got up, got my dogs, and went up this holler. There's an old house up there. So, I was up there sitting, and my dogs was down there in the big kudzu vines chasing a rabbit.

I was up there at the house, sitting on this big rock, and somebody started throwing rocks at me! I could feel it—I could hear that rock come, and I could also hear it hit the ground and bounce. At first, I thought it was my neighbors down there throwing rocks at me, but I came down to their house and I saw them out there in their yard on the porch. I come on down to the house, and I got to talking to them—the old man was raised there. And I said, "Buddy, I was hunting up there, and there was somebody throwing rocks at me."

"Oh," he said. "They ain't nothing." He said, "They've done that." Said, "I've lived here since way back when—they's a ghost up there!" Well, there's an old cemetery just down the hill from the house; they say it belongs to the Cherokee, or the Shawnee, or maybe one of the old tribes that used to live here. He said that the old-timers didn't want nobody around there because the spirits of those tribes were still in there. He said that his dogs would be laying out in the yard and said all at once't a big rock would come in right off that mountain and hit the ground, and you could hear it bounce. It was the Indian spirits, he said. He said nobody never did know where the cemetery was at.

Another time, my wife and her brother was walking down a path through the woods there. He stopped to scratch his butt, I guess, and she said that something was beginning to throw rocks at her! Said they went on and on and on, and every time you'd walk through there, they'd throw rocks at you. Now that nobody lives up there, I own two farms up there where these rocks are thrown, and since everybody's moved out of there, don't nobody hear anything no more up there.

They's another place, when I was a young man, I went fox hunting. Went up there at what they call Second Fork. I was sitting there in an old house, and nobody lived in this old house for years. But my dogs was running the fox somewhere, and all at once't, they's a big ball of fire come right out of that point, come down to that old house, and went right down into that chimney. You know what I done? I started that car up, and I left! And I ain't been back since! That's on Second Fork on Wooton. This place here where I saw these ghosts throwing rocks at me was up on what's called Bailey's Branch. The righthand fork of Bailey's Branch, they used to call it Joseph Fork.

"Witchy" George Joseph

Told by Jamie Leigh Dean. This story is dedicated to the memory of Tena Baker-Dean.

Being raised by an older generation, I grew up very old-fashioned and heard my Mommaw telling me stories from her parents and grandparents, stories that die over time from not being passed on.

One particular person she talked about was Witch George Joseph. He was our relative. He always used his powers for good, except one time. The most famous thing he was known for was putting a cow on top of the barn. A man was going to sell it, and it wasn't a cow worth selling. When the man had got up the next day, the cow was up on the top of the barn! Witch George told him he couldn't do bad and get away with it.

My great-grandma, Stella, was churning butter, and Witch George came up to her and said, "Not much milk?" and she said, "No, the cow didn't give much today." When he left, my great-grandma said she never churned so much butter in her life!

The only time he used his powers for bad was on his own son. He went to his son's house and picked out a lamb that he wanted to eat and told him to fix it the next day. When he went to his house the next day, he asked his son if that was the lamb he had picked the day prior. His son told him that it was. They all ate, and after the meal his son got sick—deathly sick. As he was laying on what would have been his deathbed, Witch George went up to him and asked his son if he had anything to confess to him, because he could "save his life." His son told him no. Witch George told his son that he knew that he had deceived him by trying to give him another lamb than the one he himself had picked out. His son died right then and there.

Gifts of this nature are passed down to each generation. Each person's gifts are unique, and a gift from God. As a descendent, I consider myself an inheritor of some of his powers, but, as a granny witch, mine are of a different nature than Witch George's. There's a lot of magical work done in these hills, and many stories are told about Witch George, but these are just a few of the ones I was told directly by my parents and grandparents who experienced them.

The Unrest of Octavia Hatcher

Told by Brittany Brock

I'll start off by saying, I'm not from Pikeville, but I had a brief obsession with the Octavia Hatcher affair years ago. Basically, in the nineteenth century Octavia was a young debutante of the Pikeville upper crust who married another very wealthy Pikevillian man named James Hatcher. In 1890, Octavia and James had a baby son, named Jacob, who died not long after he was born. As a result of her loss, Octavia went into a deep depression and stopped taking care of herself. A mysterious illness was coming through the mountains at the time, and Octavia caught it. When the doctors came by, at the request of her husband, they couldn't see or hear her breathing, or locate her heartbeat. So, they pronounced her dead. This was in May, and it was a really hot summer. So, they had to bury her right away, beside her son Jacob. Embalming techniques were rather primitive back then, and there was a great fear of the sickness spreading from her corpse.

Well, not long after her funeral—maybe two or three days—the doctors began noticing other victims of the illness had the same symptoms as Octavia and would appear lifeless but within a few days would emerge from the comatose state. While the afflicted were unconscious, their breathing became very shallow, and their heart rates dropped so low so that they couldn't hear it.

James Hatcher then began to panic, because he realized that he may have inadvertently buried Octavia alive, and called for an emergency exhumation. When they dug her up, the lining of her coffin was ripped to shreds, and her fingernails were bloody. Her face was scratched, swollen, and supposedly twisted in terror from trying to free herself. Her coffin wasn't airtight as coffins are now, so when Octavia had awoken from her illness-induced slumber, she found herself inside of a coffin, six feet underground, and naturally was filled with frenzied terror and tried to escape, in vain. This time, she was actually dead-dead. James never recovered from this; he built a hotel to overlook her grave and ended up having his own coffin on display at the establishment. His coffin, ironically, included a little bell built into the casket in case he suffered the same fate as Octavia. He never actually forgave himself for what happened.

Some people have heard what sounds like a cat screaming and crying while visiting the grave of Octavia Hatcher, which is still marked by a magnificent tombstone featuring her likeness. Others say they hear a baby crying or see a mist surrounding the grave. My favorite story is that on the anniversary of her death, her statue's head turns from one direction to the other, symbolic of her "turning her back" on Pikeville.

I've actually been to Octavia's grave site, and the air is so thick there. It's different than a humid thick. It's just heavy—like a tightness in your chest heavy. They have it gated off, but you can still see it from the grave site. When I was there, the gate wasn't locked and the door was open, which was really odd, but I went in anyway. It was almost as if she invited me in. There's pennies and toys left for Jacob, but most have weathered away. You always feel like someone is watching you, and you can sense the panic in the locale. It's as if her statue's eyes follow you through the cemetery, and she is always looking down upon the city of Pikeville. Despite going in the middle of summer, the air is always chilly, and it almost looks as if the statue has been crying, with the way the marble has faded. Sometimes, when I look at the way the marble has aged, it's as if her face shows just how genuinely terrified she must've been. It's breathtaking for sure, because you just feel so . . . sad there. I sat with her a while and just felt the wind blow. She's not an evil or hurtful spirit, but she does carry so much pain.

How to Become a Witch

Anonymous

I'd like to preface this account by saying that I cannot in good conscience recommend any of y'all try this at home—and I accept no responsibility for the consequences that may ensue if you *do* decide to try this out! That being said, these are the two "traditional" methods that I've heard whispered around these hills concerning how to become a witch—that is, gaining unearthly powers at the price of your soul—that were practiced by some in old Appalachia.

A lot of witchcraft was practiced all over southeastern Kentucky in the old days, and particularly in Leslie County. But back then, becoming a witch was not so simple of an undertaking. You couldn't simply walk into Whole Foods, buy some organic sage, burn a few candles, adopt a black kitten, and call yourself a witch. In the old days, becoming a witch involved nothing short of summoning the devil, meeting him face to face and selling your soul.

By far the most common version of how to become a witch involves the following procedure.*

1. The aspiring witch must climb to the top of a very high mountain at dawn. They need to leave early, because they need to arrive at the top before sunrise. They must take with them a firearm and bullets, a writing implement, and a large basin (most commonly made of pewter—but any would do). According to some traditions, a handkerchief may also be required, as will be explained below.
2. As the sun is rising, the would-be witch must shoot their gun directly at the rising sun. Some say you have

to shoot at the sun through a handkerchief, but I have heard both variations.
3. After firing the gun, the would-be witch must then curse the Lord and swear allegiance to the devil for the rest of their days, three times each.
4. If these parts of the operation are successfully performed, it is said that a raging storm of thunder and lightning should emerge. The wind will howl, and the earth will shake. This storm is said to be so terrifying that it would scare most of the aspirants off—sending them running off the mountain and quitting the operation prematurely. However, if the would-be witch is brave enough, they will remain standing firm throughout the storm, and place the basin on the ground.
5. It will then begin to rain blood, or a drop of blood will fall from the handkerchief, if you believe this version. If, after all this, the prospective witch continues to remain standing, the devil himself will soon appear to them with a contract, granting great powers in exchange for their immortal soul. He will stretch out his arms, placing his hands on the length of the would-be witch's body, encompassing the span of head to toe.
6. Now, if the candidate were to sign the contract with a writing instrument, using blood gathered in the basin, they would become a witch, gaining fantastic dark powers for the remaining length of their days.

Pretty scary stuff, right? Well, there were several well-known witches in Leslie County who outright told others they became a witch, or at least tried to become a witch, using this method. However, it was told that most would get so scared when the storm began to rise, they would abandon all hopes of becoming a witch and flee! Dora Fields even claimed that one of these "quitters" became one of the finest preachers in Laurel County! Talk about a career change!

*This is my paraphrasing of several versions I've heard from three different sources, which include Dora Fields's interview with Sadie W. Stidham, April 30, 1979, Frontier Nursing Service Oral History Project, Louie B. Nunn Center for Oral History, University of Kentucky Libraries; Sadie Stidham, *Trails into Cutshin Country: A History of the Pioneers of Leslie County, Kentucky* (Viper, KY: Graphic Arts Press, 1978), 119; and Daniel L. Thomas and Lucy B. Thomas, *Kentucky Superstitions* (Princeton, NJ: Princeton University Press, 1920), 277–78.

Another Formula for Becoming a Witch

Anonymous

There is also another less common method I have heard on how to become a witch. Nevertheless, I've also heard it told from other Leslie County folks, so I'll recount it for you here.*

1. The would-be witch must wake up before sunrise and walk eastward until they come to a black stump—being careful not to speak to or say a word to anyone they may encounter along the way.
2. They must then repeat this trip, seven consecutive mornings in a row, always in total silence.
3. If they are successful, the devil will appear to them on the morning of the seventh day, sitting on the stump. The would-be witch must then swear allegiance to the devil, and they will then gain the powers of a witch.

Now, I can't attest to how true *any* of these methods are, but in Leslie County alone, I know of at least two people who claimed to have attempted the first method. One was "successful" as far as I know, based on stories he told, and other people told about him, but that was well before my time. I'm not about to try it out myself, and as I said earlier, I can't recommend you do it either. I'd sure hate to meet someone who's done it and find out!

---

*I also read this version of the story in Stidham, *Trails into Cutshin Country*, 119.

The Legend of the John Asher's UFO

Told by Eric Wilder, Jonathan Wilder, Andy Wells, and Dustin Feltner. This story is dedicated to the memory of Patrick Smith, who was also a witness to the events.

One night in the late '90s or early 2000s, a group of Leslie County teenagers' weekend campout quickly became an *X-Files* episode. The following story consists of multiple accounts of a mass UFO sighting that occurred around Hay Hill in the John Asher's strip-mine area of Leslie County, Kentucky.

ERIC'S STORY

It was the early 2000s. Limp Bizkit topped the charts, Mike Jones gave everyone his phone number, it was pre-Facebook, and Snake was the best game on your black-and-white Nokia cell phone. Most importantly, we were a group of about ten to fifteen boys from southeastern Kentucky who were extremely adventurous.

We camped in a teepee that we all built on top of a mountain a couple miles above my parents' house. We would go in any weather—there was never an excuse to not go camping. After it got dark, we'd get our courage up, and usually we'd walk to the strip job a few miles across the point that locals call John Asher's. Our destination was always a mountain known as Hay Hill. I have been told Hay Hill is the highest peak in Leslie County.

Being curious teenagers, we would always talk about Bigfoot, the Blair Witch, and some local ghost stories our parents had told us. We would laugh them off and thought strange phenomenon were just stories to spark the imagination. That was, until our experience with the otherworldly on Hay Hill this particular night . . .

When we got to Hay Hill on John Asher's, we noticed the brightest light I have ever seen in the night sky. It was about as bright as the moon. We all discussed it and joked that it was a UFO and laughed it off. We accepted that since it wasn't really moving, it must just be a satellite, a planet, or a star.

After about thirty minutes, our friend Patrick (who passed away a couple years ago) said, "Guys, our star is moving!" The "light" began to move left to right and up and down. In spite of the strange movement, it still looked to us just like one light similar to a very bright star. Then, to our surprise, the "star" starts coming our way and gets much lower. As it got closer, we could see it shining a beam onto the mountaintops in front of us . . .

Not only that, we could now see more lights, triangularly shaped, on the craft. No doubt now, it was definitely a craft of some sort. Finally, it got directly above us, not very high off of the ground at all. It blacked out a spot in the sky, which I think was also triangular in shape, but it had to be nearly the size of a football field and made zero noise.

My brother, myself, and a couple of others ran to the highest peak we could, Hay Hill, so we could see more of this mysterious craft that our group of friends to this day call "the UFO." After it passed over us, it took off at a speed so fast that it's hard to explain. I don't know how something so large could move so fast. It was almost like the warp speed that you hear about on *Star Trek*.

To this day, there are so many things about this UFO sighting that can't be explained. It sat stationary in the sky thirty to forty minutes after we first noticed it. I don't know how it could have moved side to side and up and down at the rate it did. How can something so large hover so low in the sky while shining beams that illuminated the mountaintops so brightly? How was it so quiet, not making a sound as it moved? And lastly, how does something so large, or any size, move so fast? That night has connected me and the other witnesses in a special way. Every time we see each other, we always talk about it and remain puzzled as to what we saw. After more than twenty years, the conversation always ends the same way. We all agree it was nothing from this planet and reminisce about how much we miss our dear friend Pat, who first declared, "Guys, our star is moving!"

ANDY'S STORY

Twenty years is a long time to remember anything, but I remember this pretty vividly. Growing up, we would camp out a lot on top of the mountains behind our house. You know, in southeast Kentucky a lot of the mountains were strip-mined, so at nighttime we would walk around on the strip-mined mountains. And it's really clear up there you know—there's no lights. You're kind of out in the middle of nowhere; there's no streetlights or anything.

One night, we were walking on the highest point of that strip mine where we lived, a place called Hay Hill. They called it Hay Hill because they tore that whole mountain down when they strip-mined it, and it was still one of the highest points in Leslie County—anyhow, they covered it with hay to try and get the grass to grow back. The top of the mountain had a beautiful view. We were looking up at the sky that night and we saw a really, really bright star.

For what felt like the longest time, we argued over whether or not it was actually a star. Keep in mind, this was a time when drones didn't exist or if they did people didn't have 'em to play around with. Satellites move, but they never change direction—they always stay in one constant orbit or movement. It's the same with airplanes, they don't hover—well, to the best of my knowledge, they don't hover. Helicopters do hover, but they don't have bright lights like this did. Anyway, we argued over whether or not it was a star or a satellite or whatever we thought it was.

Then this "star" started moving. Real slow. It would move real slow to the left—so slow at first it was hard to tell whether or not it was actually moving. It would move really slow, back and forth, up and down, left and right . . . It was incredibly bright. Brighter than any star in the sky. Eventually, as we were arguing over what it was, it takes off over our heads as fast as I have ever seen anything in the sky take off in my life. It got brighter as it went over top of our heads, and you could kind of see more color to it as it went over. At that point, I realized it wasn't a helicopter; it would have had to have been one hell of a fast helicopter for it to be a helicopter. You know—drones didn't exist like that, and airplanes don't hover.

So, to this day, I'd say it was a flying object that I can't identify.

DUSTIN'S STORY

It was the year 2000. Or maybe it was 2001. Perhaps it was 1999. Seems like a better story if it's 1999, so we'll go with that. It was October, I think. It was cool but not cold. We were young, dumb, and a ton of fun. We were nerds, goofballs, and an odd bunch. We had a teepee.

We spent our weekends on the mountain, adjacent to the strip job, and above the kingdom of Eddie Wilder. Eddie Wilder is Jon and Eric's dad, and he cooked a mean breakfast. I will never forget his breakfast. It was epic. That's another story altogether though. On said mountain, the Wilders had constructed a teepee on a wooden platform. This is where we camped. This is where we built monstrous fires and cooked pork chops and steaks hung by sticks directly over the fire. This is where we slept in green beans. This is where we played a little paintball. This is where we had log-tossing contests, for some strange reason. It was our corner of the forest, and we liked it there.

It was Friday night, and we had all gathered at the teepee. Or maybe it was Saturday. Either way, we had discussed camping all week, and it was finally here. I was pumped. The fire was built. Miller Hi-Lifes were somewhat cold. We were good to go. We had a crew. The crew changed somewhat from week to week, so it's hard to pinpoint exactly who was there. I know that Jon, Eric, Ned, Andy, Andrew, Pat, and myself was there. Perhaps J.J. was there. Perhaps Dale was there. This night, we had decided to go walking. We had done this a time or two before, and it was a blast. Imagine being with your best friends, walking across the highest mountains around, looking at the stars and talking about anything and everything. The four-wheeler roads we walked on led to the main part of John Asher's—the legendary John Asher's strip job.

John Asher ran a sawmill at the bottom of the mountain, probably in the '70s or '80s. Who knows when. All I know is that when they decided to strip-mine the top of that mountain, and flatten it, it became known as John Asher's. Amazing views, amazing parties, and a network of dirt roads that could take you anywhere in the county. It was awesome. The most popular spot on this illustrious redneck riviera was known as Hay Hill. Sorry, *plateau*. Hay Hill was a mountain that had been cut into but not cut all the way. What was left was a steep hill and a peak at the top. It was once covered in hay to help the grass grow back, but that had long been knocked off by four-wheelers and motorcycles.

Hay Hill was our destination this night. Our trusty lanterns had led us all the way there. I'm guessing the walk was somewhere around two miles. The sky was perfectly clear. A few of us had climbed to the top. I know Pat was up there with a couple others. I was sort of midway up the hill. We were rolling down the hill. I have no idea why. I remember Pat started to talk about a light over another mountain. We all looked at it. I assumed it was a star. I continued to act foolish. At some point, we had all made it to the top. It was then that Pat said loudly in a very Pat-like tone: "Uhhh, guys, our star is moving!" Everyone froze.

Every eye was on the light that was a star but suddenly wasn't a star. I remember there was some arguments over if it was really moving. You see, at first it just moved slightly. Left to right, up and down, almost like a bobble or wiggle. It done this for a few minutes. Some people moved on to other shenanigans. Then, almost as if it needed more attention, the light really started to move. Sharp, immediate movements to the left and to the right. Unpredictable. Our attention was captured.

This thing needed zero time to change direction. That's the first thing I noticed. Not a helicopter, not a weather balloon. Years before drones were available. Instantly changing direction. What was happening? We were locked in.

It moved across the sky from mountaintop to mountaintop. It was low. At this point, we were shining our lights up at it and screaming at it like the idiots we were. A few of us swore it was a helicopter. But there was no way. There was no sound. Just movement. Then it started illuminating the mountaintops. We were sure to be abducted, and we were excited about it.

Then, as best as I can remember, it stopped. I'm not certain, but I believe it stopped as it looked at us. Had the pilot just noticed the idiots jumping on top of the mountain? It paused there for a period. Sphincters tightened. Then, our star that's not a star, in a final, radical movement, exited stage right. It "whooshed" to the right and over the mountains and it was gone. Gone-gone. Never to be seen again.

We waited. We walked around the corner of Hay Hill and waited some more. It was gone. We were speechless, amazed, somewhat scared, and pumped about it. We had seen a UFO. We had witnessed something as a group that would live on with us forever. I feel as if I'm part of a secret society. Ask any of the guys who were there that night. They will tell you, without a doubt, we saw a UFO. The walk back to camp was spent with heads up to the sky. I was sure it would come back. But it didn't. Like I said, it was gone-gone. We zipped up our green beans—yes, they are sleeping bags—and finally went to sleep. The legend of the Hay Hill UFO was born.

JONATHAN'S STORY

I will tell this the best I can remember it. It has been over twenty years since this took place, and to the best of my knowledge it probably happened in the summer of 2000 or 2001.

On any weekend when it was remotely possible, a large group of us would camp, from the beginning of the weekend after school until Sunday morning when we would all walk off the ridge we camped on, and my dad would make us breakfast. We had for years had a rough wood floor built on a ridgetop that we had formed into a rough teepee with tarps and wood beams. We would hide beer under the floor and drink it warm when we came back. We never got in any trouble, and we had a lot of freedom. Some of us would walk up to the ridge from our homes, and others would ride four-wheelers to meet us. There were more weekends like this than I can accurately recount.

On this weekend, which I cannot tell you with any specificity when exactly it was, there was a group of ten–fifteen of us. From the ridgeline where we camped, we could walk for a mile or a mile and a half and reach a very popular spot on an old strip mine immediately adjacent to us. That area was extremely popular with four-wheeler riders (in the pre side-by-side era) and partiers. The open space isolated from everything else was perfect for both. On this night, probably sometime between 10:00 and 11:00 p.m. (maybe later), the entire contingent of our group left the campsite and walked by moonlight to the most popular spot on the strip mine. It was called Hay Hill by everyone around, because when it had been most recently stripped it was covered in hay during the period of reclamation. Hay had regrown, and the steepness of the top of the hill created enough of a challenge for four-wheeler and dirt-bike riders to get a thrill. Every now and then, someone would roll off the hill, flipping backward for a couple of hundred feet. It was traversable but dangerous if you made a mistake. The air at night was warmer there. Warm air pockets would come and go, and sometimes at night it would feel nearly as warm as daytime there.

Myself, Patrick Smith, my brother Eric Wilder, Dustin Feltner, Andy Wells, Eric Whitaker, and several of the others who normally spent those weekends rambling around the woods and strip-job plateaus were there that night. We were all talking. We would get in conversations, and the group would build buzzing energy together as we laughed at whatever madness we would get going on. At the core of it, we were good friends getting to spend time together. This ended up being a weird night. We still talk about it.

At some point during a conversation, myself and Pat saw a very bright star on the horizon. We talked about it a little bit as an offshoot of some other conversation and decided it was probably a bright star. No big deal. About half an hour later, Pat looked at me and said, "I think your star is moving." I looked out to the horizon facing away from the hill, and, sure enough, it was. It had started creeping away from its position. We looked at it long enough to realize it was now moving. As we kept looking at it, it seemed to pick up speed. A lot of speed. Our bright star was something else.

We started talking as a group and curiously guessing at what it was. At some moment it would be hard to pinpoint, the group together realized this was something else than we knew. It was large, seemingly very high, and very fast. The stationary star was a fast-moving "something." As it passed over our heads, we turned to follow it. Its direction went straight over Hay Hill, and several of us ran straight up the hill to follow it as long as we could. As we were partially up the hill, it almost stopped completely, or did stop completely, and then moved completely out of our view on the skyline in an instant—literally zipped away at a speed and direction impossible. The change in direction and immediate speed almost looked like when you watch *Star Trek* and they hit warp speed, except there was a direct change in direction. We thought it was incredible. No one was scared, but we were amazed. We didn't know what we saw, but we knew with certainty it wasn't normal. Planes, helicopters, shooting stars, and anything that someone would ever try to explain this away with are things we had all seen hundreds of times. We were as experienced as anyone at identifying objects in the sky, even as teenagers. We all talked about it for years. My strongest memories from this sighting are with my great friend Patrick, who has sadly passed since that time, after a life as a podcaster, radio DJ, and author. This one is for you, buddy. Rest in peace.

V   HUMOROUS HAINTS

These stories tickle instead of terrify.

A Successful "Haint Hunt"

Told by Deron Mays

My dad was a fox hunter, and he was in the hills and hollers a lot in his life, usually camping out overnight with a group of other fox hunters. They would build a fire on a knob, high enough in elevation to hear their dogs chase the fox. They weren't interested in catching the fox, just listening to the hounds in the chase. He told me about an experience he had during one of the campouts.

> We were camped out on a hilltop and had a good fire built. We had been there several hours listening to our dogs run the fox when one of the other hunters saw something in an old church down the holler below us. The church was no longer in use and was in poor condition. My buddy kept pointing and saying, "What is that?"
>
> It was stormy-type conditions but not raining. The wind was gusting, and it was lightning. The church was next to a graveyard, and that got everyone's attention. We could see something floating inside the church, something white. We had no idea what it was.
>
> One of the men said it was a warning sign because we were camped too close to the graveyard. They were ready to pack up and leave. However, I was more curious than afraid. So I told them I was going down there to see what was going on. Well, they went nuts on me and said that I was going to bring evil spirits or something bad onto all of them. But I didn't listen and grabbed a flashlight and headed toward the church, by myself. When I finally got there, I saw that a lot of plants had grown up around the church. I waded through a thicket of briars and high

weeds to get to the front door. I opened it and went inside. And I immediately saw the ghost.

The church had a high ceiling and one big chandelier hanging from it. The windows of the church were mostly broken, and the windy conditions from the approaching storm were blowing through the openings and whistling through the building. Hanging from the chandelier was an old white curtain that had somehow gotten wrapped around it. Every time the lightning flashed, it reflected off the white curtain, which was floating up and down as the wind gusted through the windows. I stood there and let it all soak in for a minute. It was simply a natural phenomenon that was creating a ghostly image.

I went back up the hill, and the hunters were still there, which kind of surprised me, since they were the scaredy types. I told them I had found their ghost. And they were relieved when I explained what it was.

If I hadn't gone down the hill to that old church, those fellers would have told that ghostly story to anyone who would have listened, and every time it was told by them, or retold by someone they had told, it would have become bigger and embellished. That's how most ghost stories work. It's like the telephone game, never the same as the years pass.

The Pack Peddler's Bones

Told by Hobert Miniard, adapted by Matthew R. Sparks

Well there used to be a lot of pack peddlers from Germany coming through these hollers—I reckon they all came from Germany. They'd bring their stuff from over there and come to peddle it here. How did them Germans ever get over here in this country with that awful load of stuff on their back a-peddlin' on it? They'd a had to have landed in Floridy or something like that. They had the awfullest loads of stuff on earth on their backs! They'd carry so much, it would break a horse down. Pots and pans a-janglin' tied everywhere stacked five feet above their heads. I seen many of 'em go through here when I was a boy. I remember 'em mighty well. They'd walk from one house to another, stop at every house they come to, and peddle and ask if they could stay the night—I don't know much about 'em, to be honest, but they used to stay all night at Daddy's over there.

Now, this used to be a rough, and I mean rough, country. Outlaws. There was a bunch down in this holler over on Gross Branch. I reckon they used to kill everyone that went through here. I think an old peddler came over there one night, asked to stay the night, they cut his head off. Stole his entire load of goods. Some old man who lived up there ended up with the entire load of that peddler's goods on display in his store.

Them outlaws took his body down to Lewis's Creek. Right early one mornin', they's a-digging in the bank to bury him. Now, there used to be a big salt well over there on Straight Creek, and Granny Lou and them would go out across Lewis's Creek to Straight Creek there to gather salt in them days. Well, while they was a-digging a shallow grave to put the bones of that peddler in, Granny Lou was going to fetch salt and came across that bunch a-digging that hole. Well, they didn't work on the roads them days, and she didn't know what they was a-doin' at the time. Later on, when they started working on the roads, they eventually dug some of that old peddler's bones out.

There was a boy by the name of Henry Pennington, "Old Bad Henry"—he was a rough 'un—who used to live in this country. Anyway, he left here and he was gone a long, long time. He was always trouble. His Mammie, who lived here, came across that pack peddler's bones after they dug them up and thought it was Henry's bones. She was sure that someone had killed him and buried him there. Well, she come and got 'em—the bones—in her apron and took 'em home and buried 'em.

Well, a year or two after that, old Henry come in. She was a-spinnin' away on the old spinnin' wheel. He was a-talking at her, asked her if she knew him. She said, "No, I don't know you." He said, "Well, this is Henry, your son, Henry!" and the old lady fainted on the floor! When Henry came back, his mammie didn't know him, and she thought that old peddler's bones were his!

They never did find his head though. They never did figure out what happened to his head. But there used to be an old house over in Gross Branch that everyone said was hainted. People said they would always hear hollerin' and stuff over there, I don't know. Sometimes Daddy would go fishing with his brothers and their buddies, and they'd spend the night over there. One night, they was warming their feet by the fire, and all of a sudden they heard a strange noise coming from the corner of the house. They looked over, and they was a skeleton head moving all over the floor! Truthfully, I reckon a mouse or a critter had got in it or something, but that skeleton head was rolling all over, and it scared that bunch to death! They all ran out of that house, and I reckon they never went back.

I don't know what ever happened to that old house, but I do wish that old pack peddler could have had a proper burial and that those outlaws would've had the decency to give his head back!

"That's the Closest I've Come to an Encounter with a Haint!"

Told by Deron Mays

I'm sixty-eight years old, and I have never heard or seen anything unusual in my life that I didn't finally discover what it was. For instance, when I was a small boy, I slept in a room in the back of the living quarters of the county jail. By that time, my brothers had both graduated and left home, so I had the room to myself. My sisters also had a bedroom for themselves.

I was, like any child, scared of spooks and noises, as well as seeing things in the shadows at night, which was compounded by me having nearsightedness. For weeks, I had been hearing a thump, thump, thump sound. It sounded like someone knocking on a door with the back of their hand folded into a fist. The thumps would sometimes be slow, then they would pick up speed and go faster. It sounded like it was right outside my window. I would curl up under the quilts and blankets and cover my head (because all little children know ghosts, spooks, et cetera can't get to you if you're under the covers).

That noise went on all summer. Occasionally I would get the nerve to open the curtains and look out the window but never saw anything but darkness and streetlights in the distance. I mentioned it a few times to Mom and Dad, but they brushed it off as me watching too many scary movies at the local theater.

Toward the end of the summer, a time I always dreaded because it meant school would soon resume, I was outside the jail playing, and suddenly I heard the same thump sound that had terrified me all summer. I followed the sound, which is safe to do in daylight, and finally found the source. My dad had built a large doghouse just below my bedroom window. It was more the size of a smokehouse or storage house, hand-built from wood. Inside the structure were his hunting dogs, and outside was a fenced-in area for them to roam. Several dogs were inside at the time. I unlocked the gate to the fenced area and went inside and walked to the doorway of the doghouse. I stood there for a few minutes, and, sure enough, the thumping resumed. It was one of the hounds scratching himself, and every time he moved his back legs to scratch and dig, he would thump the side of the wooden building. I had to stand there a few minutes to observe, and then I started laughing. I had been scared all summer of some unknown force, and it turned out to be an old fox hound.

That's the closest I have come to an encounter with a haint, and it ended up having a natural explanation.

Paw Hensley and the Naked Haint Woman of Squabble Creek

Told by Larry Sparks, adapted by Matthew R. Sparks

My great-grandpa Hensley Sparks was a walking, talking tall tale, born and raised in Clay County, Kentucky, on what the locals called Sexton's Creek. Paw Hensley, you see, was a dry-goods salesman; he handled a variety of fabrics, sewing supplies, some clothing, and other assorted household goods. He peddled his wares for the Deaver's Dry Goods Company of Knoxville, Tennessee.

Paw's travels took him across the hills and hollers of southeastern Kentucky. Perry County, Breathitt County, Clay, Owsley, and even Leslie, wherever he needed to go to make a sale so that he could bring home as much as possible at week's end to put a big smile on my great-granny Mabel's face. When Paw first began his career as a salesman, he traveled by mule, but as roads and modes of transportation advanced, Paw found himself a 1942 Ford pickup. The old truck might as well have been made of gold in Paw's eyes. This is where our story really begins.

One late Friday afternoon in August, Paw had just dropped off a big delivery of goods to the Oneida Baptist Institute, a place dear to Paw's heart and at which he attended school for several years, until an unfortunate Halloween prank gone afoul brought about his expulsion (but that is a story for another time). Paw capped off his big sale by treating himself to a generous bowl of shucky beans laced with fresh garden green onions from Arnett's Diner—his work for the week was done. The only thing between him and home was the winding, curving, goat trail of a road between Oneida and Buckhorn.

Paw was off. Oneida, Bullskin, Saul, on to Squabble Creek. It was about right here on the edge of Saul and Squabble Creek that Paw began to crave something sweet; berries, grapes, and apples were all plentiful that time of year. Any would be nice. That's when Paw remembered a little orchard of June apple trees that were always full of apples—a nice peaceful place for a weary traveler to stretch his legs. It was settled: to the orchard for a brief stopover and a snack.

As Paw neared the orchard, it dawned on him just how close the orchard sat to the infamous Luce-Angel Graveyard. For y'ens not familiar with the area, the Luce-Angel Graveyard was a scary place. Locals as well as casual passersby had reportedly seen ghosts, goblins, witches, and boogers of all such description. It was scary enough in the daytime, but no one, I repeat, no one would be caught near the Luce-Angel at night. That being said, Paw was no coward, "he weren't afraid of no ghosts," and besides, it was late afternoon–early evening, and it would only take a few minutes to take a little apple break.

As fortune would have it, Paw spotted a June apple tree directly across the road from the entrance to the Luce-Angel. Paw pulled off the road, got out of the truck, and plucked three of the prettiest June apples you'd ever seen. He remembered how Granny Sparks used to caution his brothers and sisters to not eat too many of the June apples: as she said, they'd give you "the bellyache." Paw found him a shady spot to eat those three apples, and they were delicious!

However, going back to Granny Sparks's warning, the combination of the shucky beans and the June apples was creating quite the racket in Paw's innards. A bellyache would be putting it lightly. Paw decided he'd better get on the road, but first he was going to pick a couple of the prettiest apples off that June apple tree to take to Granny Mabel. The prettiest apples were on a high limb, but Paw was determined. He pulled his truck up underneath the bottom of the tree, climbed up on the hood, and stretched as far as he could stretch to reach those big apples.

Unfortunately, Paw stretched a little too far. In that uncomfortably stretched out position, Paw accidentally "passed a little gas." At least he thought it was gas. And it did seem to give him a little relief from his belly pains. Paw thought, "If I could only get a little bit more of that bad air out, I'd be cured." Paw then attempted to pass a little more gas. As misfortune would have it, the fart became a "shart," and Paw's favorite pair of seersucker pants were thoroughly soiled. After an outburst of words not proper for this story were let out, Paw hopped off the truck, trekked to the creek, dropped trou, and began to hand-wash his pants—one of the perks of a being a traveling salesman, an ample supply of soap was never far out of reach. He washed his pants out as best he could, wrung out the seersuckers almost to dry, and decided that there was still enough sun out to give his britches a quick sun dry. Paw carefully placed his pants on a low-hanging wild cherry limb that the sun was still beating down on. Paw, feeling much better after the accident, decided he would just take a rest for a few minutes under the shade of one of the June apple trees.

Paw Hensley then closed his eyes . . . not sleeping, just resting his eyes. As fate would have it on that late August evening, with a gentle breeze blowing, underneath the shade of that June apple tree, Paw fell fast asleep. Not just dozing, with the comforting sounds of the nearby creek, Paw Hensley went into a deep sleep. Time passed. When Paw finally woke up, the night was riding high and it was pitch black. "Oh NO! What have I done?!" he thought. "I've got to get out of here!"

"Where are my pants!!?" thought Hensley. He knew he had spread them across the limb of that wild cherry tree, but he couldn't find them, as it was now too dark to see. Imagine, if you will, the sight of my great-grandfather stark-naked from the waist down, flailing away in the middle of the forest undergrowth of southeastern Kentucky at night!

While Paw's bottom didn't have anything on it, his head was growing heavy—heavy with worry, heavy with the memories of stories about the creatures that frequented the Luce-Angel Graveyard. As I said earlier, all kinds of creatures were reported to have been seen in the graveyard. One of the most common spooks was the "Old Naked Haint Lady of the Creek." According to lore, the old lady ran the creek at night and spent her days in the dark hollers that surrounded the graveyard. Alleged eyewitnesses claimed that the old woman never wore a stitch, even in the winter, and that she never spoke but made an eerie, high-pitched call that sounded something like a screech owl. One victim of the old lady claimed that he was crossing Squabble Creek on a cold January morning while it was still dark and the creek was frozen over. When he'd gotten about halfway across, the ice on the far side of the creek started to crack. Suddenly, out of the ice leapt the old naked lady! She leapt like a bobcat at the man and got close enough to him to grab the boggin' hat off of his head! The man claimed she made that awful, ear-piercing noise, climbed out of the creek, and ran like a deer into the Luce-Angel Graveyard.

Anyway, Paw had her on his mind. He'd always heard how pale she was, sickly pale and wan, ghostly white, whiter than flour. Paw was a little shook. He was nervous, anxious, and downright a little bit scared, thinking he was just going to have to leave! Mabel would kill him when he got home, especially with no pants on. But just then, as so often happens in southeastern Kentucky in late August, there was a roar of thunder, then a lightning strike. Paw thought, maybe, just maybe that lightning might help me find my pants. The lightning, sure enough, became more frequent and was beginning to actually light up the sky a bit. Paw would wheel in a circle at every strike, trying to spot his seersuckers. Suddenly, a crash of thunder and a bolt of lightning illuminated the entire forest as though it were daytime for a few seconds—long enough for Paw to spot his seersuckers: they were high up in the middle of a big kudzu patch! He didn't know how they had gotten up there, maybe the wind, or maybe one of the haints had taken them up there while he slept. Who knew? Paw approached the kudzu and climbed on the branch of a nearby sugar maple to get a better reach for the elusive pants. Stretching, just inches away from his prize, Paw heard the undeniable sound of his branch breaking. Paw fell awkwardly into the kudzu patch, and that's when she appeared! The Old Naked Haint Woman of Squabble Creek! Or at least her spirit! When Paw hit the ground, there was a terrifying squeal, like that of a screech owl but shriller, more humanlike. A white mass of ectoplasm, or who knows what, hit him head-on in a blast of spiritual energy—or whatever haints are made of. And that horrible surreal cooing and squealing! The Naked Haint Lady of Squabble Creek had gotten ahold of him good!

"Forget the pants, Lord; just let me get out of here!" Paw screamed as he ran stark-flaming naked to the red Ford pickup. He said James Bond would have been proud of how he dove straight through that pickup window. Paw grabbed the key off the dash, fired up the truck, and, in his words, broke the land speed record as he made his way down Squabble Creek to Buckhorn, all the time thinking, "Lord, get me home! And what will I tell MABEL!?"

By the time Paw got to Buckhorn it was almost 10:00 p.m. He was three or four hours late, and Granny Mabel would not be happy at all. Paw had come in late before for one reason or another, and Mabel would sometimes be a little hot. But he'd always had pants on . . . this wasn't going to be good. As he rounded the curve to the house, he could see that the porch light was on and Mabel was sitting in her favorite rocker out on the porch . . . waiting.

Hensley pulled into the driveway, rolled down his window. "Howdy, Mabel," he said.

"You're late, Hensley!"

"Yeah, Mabel, I sure am," Hensley replied. "You're not going to believe what I've been through!"

"Probably won't, but it's not going to compare to what you're going to go through! Get out of that truck!"

"About that," Hensley said. "Mabel . . . about that—"

"GET IN THIS HOUSE, HENSLEY!" Mabel said. Paw sheepishly got out of the truck, carefully moving so as not to expose any more of himself than necessary and covering the most private of his parts with his fishing hat. When Hensley got within a good eyeshot, Mabel almost gave herself whiplash as she turned her head not once, not twice, but three times before screaming, "HENSLEY!! WHERE ARE YOUR PANTS?!"

"Mabel, let me EXPLAIN!" Hensley said.

"EXPLAIN TO THE COUCH!" Mabel screamed as she went to her bedroom and slammed the door behind her hard enough to make the church bells in the town ring.

Saturday morning didn't begin as a walk in the park for Paw Hensley. Great-granny Mabel had gotten up early as usual, made coffee, and prepared herself for the day. Mabel was the proprietor of Buckhorn general store, Sparks Trading Post. Mabel's family had been in the mercantile business since the turn of the century, and she could be found in that establishment six days a week. She closed on Sunday, of course, but other than Christmas, Easter, and Thanksgiving, she was there, sitting behind the counter and serving the residents of the community, with the hopes, of course, of turning a small profit along the way.

Hensley had experienced a rough night. Might have been the shuckies, might have been the June apples, might have been the Naked Lady of the Creek, might have been a combination of all, but let it be said that he hadn't gotten much rest, at any rate. To give him credit, though, he rose from his night on the couch with great enthusiasm, easing his way to the kitchen for a cup of Mabel's coffee, only to find an empty pot. Hensley knew he'd smelled coffee earlier. "Mabel!" he called. "Where's the coffee?"

Mabel walked into the kitchen and said, "Good question, Hensley. Maybe you can find some where you left your pants!" Hensley had really hoped to get a little coffee into his system before he began his grand defense, but he decided that there's no time like the present. Paw then proceeded to recount the events from the previous night. Mabel took it all in, but not without many a headshake and an eye roll. When Hensley had concluded his Perry Mason–worthy testimony, Mabel said, "Do you really expect me to believe this?"

"Mabel, it's the truth!" Hensley replied.

"Prove it, then," Mabel said matter-of-factly. "I want to see this June apple orchard that sits right across from the Luce-Angel Graveyard, and if we're lucky maybe that Naked Lady will make another appearance!"

"Let's go!" Hensley said.

The two of them loaded up in Hensley's truck and headed down Squabble Creek. The trip up the creek wasn't as unpleasant as Hensley had feared. They discussed the folk on the creek as they passed by their places. Mabel would compliment their gardens or flowers. Paw, being an avid hunter and fisherman, would point out every place he'd killed a squirrel or rabbit—or caught a fish. The time passed quickly, and before long you could see in the distance the big, hand-carved sign marking the entrance to the Luce-Angel Graveyard.

"It is a scary place," even Mabel was forced to admit. Paw eased past the entrance and there it was, the June apple orchard in all its glory.

"See, Mabel, I told you there was a June apple orchard!" Hensley said.

"Hensley, I never doubted that there was a June apple orchard, I just don't see how these June apples caused you to lose your pants!" Mabel retorted.

Hensley pulled off to the side of the road by the orchard and the two hopped out. "Here, Mabel, *here*—this is where I fell asleep; and look *here*," Hensley said as he picked up the remains of an apple core, what was left of yesterday's snack.

"OK," Mabel said, "I'll give you that, Hensley, but where's your pants?"

Hensley slowly turned in a circle, surveying the area. "My pants, sugar blossom, are right there!" Hensley was pointing toward the heap of kudzu where he had again located his pants, so unfortunately taken from him the night before—the same spot in which the Naked Lady had appeared. "There, Mabel, there, see! I told you; I *told* you!" Mabel had meandered over to the kudzu.

"Well, Hensley, maybe you weren't lying about the pants, but the Naked Lady, really?"

"I'm telling you, Mabel, I'm *telling you*, I was just about to reach my pants and the Naked Lady rose out of the kudzu with a whole host of haints and witches and boogers and goblins, all of 'em took hold of me with an energy I've not seen since we went to that snake-handling church!"

"Okay, okay, if you say so. Now get something and get those pants down. Seersuckers don't run cheap!" Mabel said.

The kudzu was high, and Paw's pants were right at the top of the patch. He said, "Mabel, if I climb that sugar maple up to that big branch there, I believe I can shimmy down on that limb and reach them."

"Ain't that what got you in trouble last night, old man?" Mable replied.

"Yes, but in the daylight, I'll be okay!" Hensley said.

So, there he went. Paw climbed out on that tree like a lumberjack, made his way to the big limb, and began to ease his way out over the kudzu pile to his now infamous seersucker britches. Hensley had made it to within arm's reach of the pants, when, just like last night—

CRACK!

POP!

THWACK!

Back into the kudzu pile he went!

As Paw's body plowed through the thick, leafy green kudzu vines, the strangest thing happened. With the flutter of what must have been a thousand wings, the awfullest bunch of mourning doves rose in unison out of the kudzu! What a spectacle it was! Those birds flapping, squealing, cooing!—a scene the likes of which Great-granny Mabel had never seen!

"HENSLEY!" Mabel yelled out. "Are you alright!?"

"Yes . . . I think so," Paw said.

"Hensley, you reckon that Naked Lady you saw last night, the ghostly pale spirit that engulfed you making all those strange scary noises, might just have been a flock of these mourning doves?"

Humorous Haints 179

As Paw fought his way out of the kudzu, holding a dead mourning dove in each hand, he replied, "Ya know, Mabel, it might have been!"

"Hensley... Hensley..." Mabel shook her head.

Hensley walked over to Mabel and gave her a big hug. "It's all good! We're having doves for dinner!"

Afterword

To live close to nature is to live close to death. It's something that every rural living individual is vaguely aware of at all times. It's something I, like most mountain children, learned before I could read—from watching my father come home with a bushel of squirrels to reeling in my first bluegill on the sandy banks of the camping area we used to frequent on Stinnett. That constant balance weaves its way into the tapestry of a person, into a community, its history. I've often believed this is why stories of haints and boogers, "booger tales" as my papaw calls them, were so pervasive in my upbringing.

There's always a spot where *something* happened. Whether it was a murder or natural disaster, something happened, and someone remembers it. It's by the nature of living close to that life–death balance that we remember and pay attention to it; by that same merit, we love to tell people about it. Sometimes it's cautionary, being told to young'uns so they don't suffer the same fate as some unfortunate soul. Sometimes it's a way to keep history from being forgotten. Sometimes, I think, people tell their stories to deal with their own ghosts. So often during this process, people would tell of something absolutely world-shattering, followed quickly by the impossible, and they would tell it with complete sincerity, sometimes as if they couldn't believe it themselves.

I think it's human nature to want to preserve yourself as much as possible; we grasp at immortality at any chance we can get. We have children and make a big deal over how much they resemble their parents and grandparents. Our worldly possessions are divvied up in preemptive wills so that the things we once owned may have second lives with those we hope will appreciate them.

Preserving our experiences through stories, such as the ones in this book, is another way of becoming immortal, through both individuals saying, "I was there" and writers recording the folkloric landscape of a region in print.

The essence of a ghost is the experience of something from the past as if it were the present. In that way, I experience ghosts every time I go back home, like most people. I walk with family down by the river and see abandoned stringers and washed-out car husks and can see the ghosts of summers spent fishing and open-windowed joyriding. I see the ghost of my father in my son's face. If you drive into the hills and get to talking with someone at the right time in the right place, there's a chance they'll experience a ghost, too, and tell you all about it.

Olivia Sizemore

Acknowledgments

The very existence of haint tales, booger tales, and the like would be impossible without the colorful collection of hill folk who remember and recount them over generations. The creation of *Haint Country* was the result of the cumulative efforts of a great community of Appalachian storytellers, some of whom are featured in this book and others who have left more of a spiritual mark on this work. This collection is first for them, as without their dedication to Appalachia and their love for the craft, this book would quite literally not have been possible. Second, we thank the staff at the University Press of Kentucky, especially Abby Freeland and Natalie O'Neal, who not only took a leap of faith with this project but remained unflinchingly supportive throughout the challenging process of carrying it to fruition. In a similar vein, we also thank folklorist Jordan L. Lovejoy for being one of the first to read our manuscript and to offer an assessment of the work's academic merits in the foreword. We give a very special thank you to everyone and anyone who's told us such stories over our youth and instilled that care in us. This includes (in egalitarian alphabetical order) Alene Bowling, Anita Fox, the late Carl "Junior" Fox, Kevin Gardner, Fred Lewis, Ulene Lewis, Jean McDaniel, Nathan McDaniel, Marilyn Montalvo, Miranda Ross, Byron Sizemore, Gail Sizemore, Thomas Sizemore, the late H. C. Sparks, Larry Sparks, Mary Ann Sparks, Melissa Sparks, and Opal, Morgan, and Tanner Thompson (and the rest of the Thompson crew). Likewise, we extend a very special thank you to the artistic forebears of this book, and a large part of our inspiration, Stephen Gammell and Alvin Schwartz for *Scary Stories to Tell in the Dark* (New York: Harper & Row, 1981), and Ruth Ann

Musick for *The Telltale Lilac Bush and Other West Virginia Ghost Stories* (Lexington: University Press of Kentucky, 1965). Thank you for pushing the bar of folk horror and horror illustration. We are standing on your shoulders with this work.

A number of other individuals have also played roles in critiquing the book as well as the artwork and maintaining enthusiasm for it in wider circles than we could manage on our own. These folks are too numerous to count, but we would like to go ahead and name a few of them (again alphabetically): Tracy Banks-Shepherd, Marion Beaucourt, Brittany Brock, Marsheena Brock, Destiny Caldwell, Kendra Cole, Cody Coots, Candi Crawford, Shania Davidson, Rashad Harrington, Miryam Jackson, Destiny Kaplan, Alnour Khaled, Yael Lavon, Zane McNeill, Sydney Meade, Scott Melton, Hannah Morgan, Keisha Morgan, Ladetra Morgan, Stephanie Morgan, Simo Mouhib, Menachem "Meni" Nizri, Mike Overbee, Anne Shamir, Yazan Taddani, Roseanne Terrill, Rhonda Turner-Meade, and Hayley Wells. Y'all believed in us from the outset and, more importantly, inspired us with your passion for this book. Your enthusiasm lit our way through the darkest hollers of haint country when even we were not so sure of how we'd get out of the woods in one piece. Thank you all from the bottom of our hearts; this book is as much yours as it is ours. It's a long road with many hands to compile and illustrate a collection of stories like this, and it wouldn't exist without your contributions. We're beyond happy to enjoy this little piece of immortality with you. Here's to y'all.

Compendium

A reference for additional information concerning the geography, lore, and storytellers that comprise this collection.

HAINT TALES

The Last Miner of Hurricane Creek: Scott Melton is a lifelong resident of Leslie County, Kentucky. Scott is well known in the community for having told this tale, usually to groups of his high school students, for years. The Hurricane Creek Mine disaster occurred on December 30, 1970, at Finley Mines 15 and 16 on the eponymous Hurricane Creek in Leslie County. Thirty-eight miners were killed as a result of the explosion, and a monument to their memory was erected in 2011 at the Hurricane Creek Mine Memorial on the site of the Finley Mine. Scott's original sighting occurred on the Wendover side of the creek, just past the site of the old mine. Others have claimed to have experienced similar phenomena along this road, as well as in an area known as The Fan on the eastern part of Hurricane Creek, toward Wooton, and the Old Road to Hazard in Perry County.

A Harlan County Séance: This story takes place in the town of Baxter, in Harlan County, Kentucky. Harlan is especially known for violence having taken place during the coal wars, earning it the nickname Bloody Harlan. Accidents involving trains were historically very common during coal mining's heyday, as the locomotives were used to transport black gold from the mines to processing facilities.

The Headlight Haint: Sizerock is a community in western Leslie County, near the Leslie–Clay County Line.

The Phantom Playmate: US Route 421 is a highway that runs north–south through most of Leslie County before turning west in the city of Hyden in parallel with the Hal Rogers Parkway. The location of the old house is impossible to verify, as it is no longer standing.

"It Was Always On When They Needed It Most": The events of this story took place in Leslie County.

The Snowy Night Visitation: The events of this story took place in Leslie County.

The Ghost of Fish Creek: Fish Creek is a small creek in Owsley County, just north of the town of Booneville, the Owsley county seat.

"Robert": The events of this story took place in Leslie County.

The Dance: The Old Buck Bridge was a truss bridge on Old Buck Road spanning the Middle Fork of the Kentucky River in Breathitt County, located southwest of the city of Jackson. According to recent reports, it has since been replaced with a modern bridge.

The Man in Black: Bear Holler is a community along the Rockhouse Creek of Leslie County, southwest of the city of Hyden. Bear Holler is said to be the site of much paranormal phenomena in the county, and many in the area have also claimed to have seen the mysterious Man in Black.

Babies under the Floorboards: The events of this story took place on the second fork of Bailey Branch, in Wooton, Leslie County, Kentucky. Donald "Dan" Caudill wrote about the subject of

Hanner Browning in his memoir *Mountains, Moonshine, and Memories* (Bremen, KY: Echo Fields Publishing, 2004), though he did not mention her by name. Interestingly, though the story beats are different, the original storyteller for both of these retellings seems to be Rhoda "Rhodie" Baker, wife of Arch Baker, who owned the land at the time. Relatives say Rhodie was a granny woman and the person who found the box of baby bones as well as attended Hanner's funeral. As of writing, we could find no records of a Hanner Browning.

The Old Owsley County Jail: The old Owsley County Jail building no longer serves as the county jail, having been replaced by the Three Forks Regional Jail in Beattyville, Lee County, Kentucky. Nevertheless, the county still uses the old building, which now houses the offices of the Owsley County Conservation District, a subdistrict of the Land Conservation Assistance Network (LandCAN). The Depression-era edifice, built from local sandstone (quarried from the same location as the stone used to build the old elementary school gym), stands on its original location on Jockey Street in Booneville. Although Jockey Street isn't listed on Google Maps (for reasons unknown), indeed, the street still bears the same name, and is the legal police address of LandCAN.

The Ghost Light: This story takes place near Portal 31 in Lynch, Kentucky, in Harlan County, which is now a museum. At one time, Lynch boasted the largest coal camp in the country and was known for the US Coal & Coke Company's hostility toward unions, contributing to the county's aforementioned moniker, "Bloody Harlan."

The Bloodstained Mother of Bailey Branch: This story takes place in the Bailey Branch area of Wooton, Leslie County, Kentucky. The authors have been unable to confirm the condition of the old schoolhouse and the well; however, it is quite likely that they are in a dilapidated state if they are still standing.

The Crying in the Night: This story takes place in Stinnett, Kentucky, on the 406 highway before Little Stinnett on the creek side.

"Yoo-Hoo, Mary Jane!": Memoirs about a Haint: This story, originally a written account, has been only slightly adapted by the authors for inclusion in this book. Sharon Gibson McIntosh is a published author and has read her narrative of this haunting for students at Owsley County High School and others on numerous occasions. Mary Jane Fox's gravestone indeed still stands on the family property.

BOOGERS

That's How Grandpa Quit Gambling: The events of this story took place in Floyd County, Kentucky.

"They Could Hear It Scream": This story takes place in Wooton, Kentucky, on Cane Branch. There are stories of big cats, panthers or "painthers," going back to when eastern Kentucky was first being settled—a trend that still persists today. To be sure, solid black-color mountain lions can occur naturally due to a condition called melanism. However, there have been no verifiable mountain lion sightings recorded in Kentucky since 1899.

The Hellacious Beast of Wild Dog Road: Wild Dog Road and Hollins Fork are two branches off Kentucky Highway 1482, "Bob's Fork Road" located in the Big Creek area of western Leslie County, Kentucky, near the Clay County line. The story is a popular local legend and the subject of many tall tales and jokes as well.

Boogers of Harvey Bend, Parts 1 and 2: The Sasquatch of 476 and the Lady in White: Harvey Bend is a stretch of Highway 476 in the Hardshell community of Breathitt County, Kentucky. The stretch is roughly demarcated by two of the Harvey family cemeteries on opposite sides of the well-known stream of Troublesome Creek, which runs parallel to the highway for most of its length. Harvey Cemetery #1 is located at the top of a hill on the north-facing side of the creek and is invisible from the highway. Harvey Cemetery #2 is located within the curve of the Harvey Bend stretch of highway and is visible from the road. According to our storyteller, the sightings of the Sasquatch creature have occurred all up and down the length of 476, while the sightings of the Lady in White took place within Harvey Bend itself. While telling these stories, our source even demonstrated to us exactly where the Lady in White had been seen along the riverbank of Troublesome Creek as it enters Harvey Bend.

"Cornhusk": The events of this story took place in Berea, Kentucky. Brushy Fork is a wooded area with multiple trails that is overseen by the college and butts up against the mountain chain on one side with the flat Alumni Field on the other. It is a popular location with students due to its proximity to Berea College campus and wooded environment.

"Big Redeye": This story was originally told by the grandfather of the contributor, Levi Lewis. The events described are said to have occurred at the top of Owl's Nest Mountain in Leslie County, Kentucky.

The Fourseam "Thing": The events of this story took place in Fourseam, Kentucky, in Perry County.

The Phantom Beast of Cow Creek: This story was adapted from a written account. Cow Creek is a community located on Highway 28 between Buckhorn, in Perry County, and Booneville, in Owsley County. Cow Creek proper, the creek itself, is located just southeast of Booneville.

The Lurker in the Cave: As discussed in the story, the precise location of the cave is impossible to verify. However, Rockcastle County and Laurel County are two adjacent central-southeastern Kentucky counties. Also mentioned in the story is Exit 49 off US Interstate 75 toward Livingston and East Bernstadt. Livingston is located in Rockcastle County, while East Bernstadt is in Laurel County. The running water mentioned in the story could have been the Rockcastle River or one of the several smaller creeks in the vicinity of East Bernstadt.

STAINED EARTH

"I Know There Are Spirits There": By the late 1800s, Bowlingtown was already a thriving community in Perry County, Kentucky. However, in 1960, Bowlingtown's residents were uprooted to make way for the planned construction of the Buckhorn Dam. After the relocation of the residents, the area was eventually flooded, creating Buckhorn Lake. The communities of Saul and Mudlick are made up of many of the descendants of former Bowlingtown residents. Saul, Mudlick, and Graveyard Point are all located in the mountains surrounding the lake along Saul-Mudlick Road. The Spruce-Pine Government Cemetery, also known as the Couchtown Cemetery, is located in nearby Buckhorn, Kentucky, in Perry County.

Tales from Bonnyman Coal Camp: The events of this story took place in the now defunct Bonnyman Coal Camp in Perry County, Kentucky, which was run by the Crawford Coal Corporation. According to the University of Kentucky's Appalachian Center, the camp itself is destroyed but the unincorporated area still has residents.

The Restless Spirits of Beech Fork Elementary School: Beech Fork Elementary School, previously known as Beech Fork Settlement School, is located in the Helton community of Leslie County about eighteen miles south of Hyden along Highway 421. Work on the school began in 1924, and although the school closed in 2004, the buildings and grounds have since been repurposed as a community center for senior citizens. Haint tales about Beech Fork school are very well known in the community. One of the compilers (Matthew) has heard stories circulated about the school since the mid- to late 1990s. As Samantha stated, even after the school closed, the rumors of hauntings and general otherworldly happenings have persisted.

My Haunted Double-Wide: The haunted double-wide referenced in this tale is the private home of the storyteller, located in War Branch, a community in southern Leslie County, Kentucky.

The Old Hyden Elementary Gym: The events of this story took place in Hyden, Leslie County, Kentucky. The old Hyden Elementary Gymnasium in downtown Hyden is particularly notable for temporarily holding the bodies of thirty-eight men who perished during the Hurricane Creek Mine disaster of 1970. The bodies were reportedly laid wall to wall while people tried to identify the individuals. Since then, the gym has reportedly been an uneasy place for those who enter.

"Sam": The log cabin referenced in the story is located in the East Bernstadt community of Laurel County, Kentucky. Information about the exact location of the house and its current owners is unknown.

"A Soul Left to Wander": Since the old Hyden Elementary Gym was used to hold the bodies of those who fell victim to the Hurricane Creek Mine disaster, many hauntings have been associated with the gym and adjacent building, formerly known as Hyden Elementary School.

Haunted Antebellum Property in Jackson County: Jackson County is in central-southeastern Kentucky, with McKee as its county seat. The precise location of the property and the current state of the buildings is unknown.

"Evil Hanner" and the Legend of Blood Rock: See "Babies under the Floorboards."

The Spirit Drums: According to the storyteller, the farmland on which the spirit drums were heard was located in the vicinity of Tyner in Jackson County, Kentucky.

The Wrong Side of the Law: The Saltwell Cemetery, also known as the Morgan Family Cemetery, is located just across the road from Stinnett Elementary School, south of Hoskinston, Kentucky. The cemetery marking the original burial place of the family in the Lower Middlefork area no longer exists.

Chaney's Knob: Chaney's Knob is located along the Rockhouse Creek area of Leslie County. US Highway 421 branches off onto Cain's Fork Road, and Chaney's Knob is at the top of the hill. As told in the story, local legend holds it that Chaney's Knob is the place where the eponymous Chaney lived and murdered her stepchildren.

HIGH STRANGENESS

"A Thinness, Where Things Can Bleed Through": This story took place on Cane Branch in Wooton, Kentucky. The storyteller off-handedly mentioned that they believed the spirit of Witch George Joseph, a late relative, was still hanging around the area, causing the phenomenon, "fooling the devil in death." A relative alluded to his old homestead having been where the current house now sits.

The Hairy Arm: Raccoon Creek or "Coon Creek" is a branch off of Cutshin Road in eastern Leslie County, Kentucky, located roughly between the communities of Smilax, Cinda, and Wooton.

"Do You See That?": London, a city in Laurel County, Kentucky, is a popular destination for many people who grew up deeper in eastern Kentucky to relocate to as working adults. It is very common for people from around the region to spend weekends and holidays with relatives there.

"You'd Think There'd Be Blood Somewhere": The events of this story took place in Leslie County, Kentucky.

Being a Caul Bearer: Being born with a caul, or membrane, over the face has long been rooted in superstition. Said to have one foot in this world and one in the afterlife, babies born as caul bearers are believed to have multiple psychic abilities. A popular example of this is mentioned in Stephen King's *The Shining.* Fans of British literature may also recall that the titular David Copperfield of the Charles Dickens classic was also a caul bearer.

"And I Ain't Been Back Since!": Floating orbs, or ghost lights, are a common thread in folklore of the Appalachians, as well as for the southern United States as a whole.

"Witchy" George Joseph: A relative of "Witchy" George Joseph told this tale. There are many stories told about George Joseph in the Wooton area of Leslie County, where George and his family lived. One of the compilers, Matthew R. Sparks, is also related by marriage to George Joseph, and his grandmother told him stories of many of George's "witchy" antics. Matthew has also written academic articles about George Joseph and the phenomenon of male witches, faith healing, and midwifery in Leslie County in the nineteenth and twentieth centuries. See Matthew R. Sparks, "The 'Charm Doctors' of Leslie County: Oral Histories of Male Witches, Midwives, and Faith Healers in Leslie County, Kentucky 1878–1978," *Bulletin of the Transilvania University of Brasov* 12, no. 61 (2019): 123–40.

The Unrest of Octavia Hatcher: The events of this story took place in Pikeville, Kentucky. Octavia is interred at the Pikeville Cemetery.

How to Become a Witch and *Another Formula for Becoming a Witch:* These narratives are drawn from a combination of local folklore, oral history, and written records.

194   Compendium

The Legend of the John Asher's UFO: John Asher's is a strip job in eastern Leslie County in the vicinity of the Rockhouse and Stinnett communities. The area is locally famous for camping, trail-riding, and partying. Hay Hill is an easily recognizable geographic feature, marked with numerous tire tracks and standing at a higher elevation than much of the surrounding mountains.

HUMOROUS HAINTS

A Successful "Haint Hunt": The events of this story took place in Owsley County, Kentucky.

The Pack Peddler's Bones: This story was originally told by Hobert Miniard of Leslie County, the great-great-grandfather of compiler Matthew R. Sparks. Matthew adapted this account from a cassette-tape recording of Hobert telling the story, which was given to him by his grandmother, Hobert's granddaughter. The unquiet ghosts of murdered German or Jewish pack peddlers is a very old, common trope found throughout the folklore of southeastern Kentucky and, more broadly, rural Kentucky in general.

"That's the Closest I've Come to an Encounter with a Haint!": This story takes place at the old Owsley County Jail, on Jockey Street in Booneville, the county seat. As mentioned, the old jail building still stands in the same location, now used by the Owsley County Conservation District.

Paw Hensley and the Naked Haint Woman of Squabble Creek: This story is written from the perspective of compiler Matthew R. Sparks, although its composition is largely the work of his father, Larry Sparks. It is an adapted version of a story that Larry told Matthew when he was a small boy, often while traveling along Squabble Creek, and the two have worked to reproduce it here. Squabble Creek is a community in Buckhorn, Kentucky, that runs parallel from Saul-Leatherwood along the edge of Buckhorn Lake State Resort Park into the Buckhorn city limits. While very much a tall tale, the story contains some elements of truth. All of the people and places mentioned in it are real, and Paw Hensley and Mabel Sparks were, in fact, characters as portrayed. The Luce-Angel Graveyard, also in Squabble Creek, has enjoyed a long reputation of being a "hainted" spot. While much of the rest of the story is embellished, Paw Hensley did once claim to have seen a naked woman bathing in a creek at night on one of his trips back home from selling dry goods. It is quite likely this incident happened somewhere in Perry County, but wherever it was, it spooked Paw Hensley so bad that he didn't like to talk about it very much—thus, a more humorous version of the tale was born.

About the Authors

Amberly Dicey

Matthew R. Sparks holds a PhD in Middle East studies from Ben Gurion University of the Negev in Beersheva, Israel. A native of southeastern Kentucky, Matthew is a published writer and researcher, focusing on minority ethnic and religious communities in the Middle East. Matthew is trained in historical anthropology methods, such as oral history, and is currently finishing a major project on the Bedouin of South Sinai, Egypt, and the Naqab desert. He has published two articles on this subject as well as articles about male midwifery and witchcraft in Appalachia and the effects of COVID-19 policies on Islamic burial practices. *Haint Country* is his first major foray into the folklore of his home region.

Caroline Benedum

Olivia Sizemore is an Appalachian artist born and raised in Leslie County, Kentucky. She holds a BA in studio art (painting) from Berea College and has worked at Nativibes Gallery in Mannington, West Virginia, while amassing a niche group of followers for her digital art side project.